Sharon Stewart

DATE DUE

JAN 3 0 2002		
JAN 3 0 2002		
APR 2 4 2002		

Scholastic Canada Ltd.

Toronto New York London Auckland Sydney
Mexico City New Delhi Hong Kong

Scholastic Canada Ltd.
175 Hillmount Road, Markham, Ontario, L6C 1Z7

Scholastic Inc.
555 Broadway, New York, NY 10012, USA

Scholastic Australia Pty Limited
PO Box 579, Gosford, NSW 2250, Australia

Scholastic New Zealand Limited
Private Bag 94407, Greenmount, Auckland, New Zealand

Scholastic Ltd.
Villiers House, Clarendon Avenue, Leamington Spa,
Warwickshire CV32 5PR, UK

Canadian Cataloguing in Publication Data

Stewart, Sharon (Sharon Roberta), 1944-
My Anastasia

ISBN 0-590-51511-X

I. Title.

PS8587.T4895M9 1999   jC813'.54   C99-30549-2
PZ7.S73My 1999

5 4 3 2 1   Printed in Canada   9/9 0 1 2 3 4/0

To the memory of OTMA and Alexei.
And to Roderick, for all the reasons.
— S. S.

1

Pokrovskoe

August, 1911

I woke shivering, and for a moment I couldn't remember where I was. My bones still ached from the beating Big Ivan had given me last night. Then I felt the prickle of straw beneath me and heard the soft huff of the cow's breath as she chewed her cud. I was in the barn. Rubbing my eyes, I sat up and wrapped my ragged shawl more closely about me. The sky was white with dawn and our cranky old rooster was crowing from the broken fence around the hen coop. I'd better be out of the way before Big Ivan got up, I thought, or he might take his stick to me again.

Big Ivan was my father, but I wouldn't call him that anymore. Not since he'd taken to beating me. When my mother was alive, it hadn't been like that. She'd known how to soften his hard heart, make him laugh, and she'd bound the three of us together with the magic web of her stories. But last winter had been wolf cold, and she had begun to cough. Though she

1

had tried to keep going, at last she took to her bed. She burned with fever, and her beautiful black hair became dull and matted as she tossed and moaned. I bathed her face and tried to make her sip a little broth, but she couldn't. One day she didn't even know me. The next day . . .

My father buried my *matushka* under the old apple tree without even so much as a priest to bless her. After that he spent every night at the tavern, stumbling in at dawn — when he came home at all. The work of the farm went undone. And when I tried to tell him stories to make him feel better, he hit me. One day he simply disappeared. The neighbours looked at me slyly out of the corners of their eyes, but said nothing. So I fed the chickens and the pig and the cow, and waited and waited. It was spring now, and the fields had to be tilled and sown if we were not to starve next winter. But how could I plough? Big Ivan had taken our old horse. At last I wrestled the small plough into a wheelbarrow, and trundled it out to the fields. I harnessed myself to it and tried to pull it, but it wouldn't budge. I sat down and cried.

But the morning is wiser than the evening. The next day I took a stick and a sack of buckwheat out to the fields. I poked holes in the ground and dropped grains of buckwheat in. The sun burned down on me, and our ragged little fields suddenly seemed as wide as the whole world.

I had sat down to rest when I heard voices and the clink of harness. A wagon was coming up the muddy road. My father was driving it, and beside him sat a strange woman. I ran over and climbed the fence.

"Sitting and doing nothing, Dunia?" Big Ivan said, frowning, as they came up to me. "A fine impression you'll make on your stepmother!"

Stepmother! She looked me up and down, the cat-eyed one. "Dirty," she sniffed. Then she looked around the farmyard, at the sagging barn and our tumbledown *isba*. "What a liar you are, Ivan," she complained. "A fine farm, you told me you had. If I'd known *this* was what you were bringing me to, you'd have had a different answer when you proposed!"

My father shrugged, and set about unhitching the horse.

I dogged their heels as they walked toward the isba. "I *did* work!" I cried. "I fed the chickens. And the pig and cow!"

"Be quiet!" ordered my stepmother.

Folk say that in every evil there is something good — but I could find none of it in *her*. It was "Do this, Do that" all day long, and always the dirtiest, nastiest tasks, too. At first I tried to please her, but when I couldn't, I didn't try anymore. I shirked my chores whenever I could, hiding myself away where she couldn't find me. Sometimes I'd climb the apple tree over my mother's grave, and tell her the stories she had told me long ago, tales of onion-domed cities, golden palaces, firebirds, flying ships.

My favourite now was "Vasilissa the Fair," because she was brave, and because she had a wicked stepmother who got what she deserved in the end.

When my stepmother couldn't find me, she complained to Big Ivan, who would take his stick to me. Last night she had turned me out of the house. "No work, no bed," she said.

The sun was peeping over the horizon now. If I fed the chickens, would my stepmother give me breakfast? Sighing, I got up. If only my mother had left me a magic doll like Vasilissa's to do all my work for me! Tania, my father's favourite wolfhound, came over, lazily wagging her tail. *She* got meat every day, and milk too. But I gave her narrow head a pat anyway. It wasn't her fault that Big Ivan didn't love me.

When I told my stepmother I'd fed the chickens, she just pursed her lips. "Very well. Do the rest of your chores, then, and perhaps you'll have bread and soup for dinner."

"But I'm hungry *now!*" I wailed. She just turned her back and went into the isba.

Well, you can't get honey from wasps. I swept the barn, and after that I weeded the cabbages. I was trudging along the dusty path to the pigpen, telling myself a story to keep from thinking how hungry I was, when something made me stop and put down the bucket of swill. The sun hung over the forest like an apple of gold, and I closed my eyes, feeling its friendly warmth. Then suddenly, as if by magic, my feet began to carry me away. I looked down at them, spellbound, as they took step after step. They seemed to know where they were going.

I was halfway across the buckwheat field before my stepmother spied me. "Dunia, you lazy brat!" she bawled. "You haven't finished your chores." Her words buzzed about my ears. "Come back this minute, or your father will take his stick to you again!"

I kept walking.

"If you run off, don't think we'll take you in again!"

I don't care. I'm never coming back, I told myself, suddenly quite sure. Not *ever*.

"You'll die in the woods! The wolves will gnaw your bones!"

Maybe they won't, I told myself. And let my brave feet carry me under the eaves of the forest.

Now, five days later, they carried me out again into a wonderful place. The village had a tall white church with gilded onion domes like the ones in my stories. The main street had hardly any potholes and was lined on both sides with neat log isbas. Even the pigs and chickens looked fat and prosperous. Hungry, I begged a crust from an old *babushka*. The sun was already below the horizon and there was a chilly breeze, so I looked around for a place to sleep, sneaking around the backs of several isbas and trying the doors of sheds and barns. All were locked.

At last I came to a large isba on the edge of the village. There was no shed behind it, just a large and smelly dung-heap. But right against the back wall of the isba lay a row of empty barrels. With a quick glance to make sure no one had seen me, I crept inside one. The barrel smelled of pickled cabbage, but at least I was out of the wind. Wrapping my shawl around me, I gnawed my crust. Then I curled up and began to tell myself a story about a brave girl who went out into the world to seek her fortune.

I had just begun to drowse when there was a loud burst of laughter from the isba. It must be a tavern, I thought sleepily. Then the laughter turned to shouts and cursing, and the back door was flung open. I peered out just in time to see a man reel across the yard and land with a thump on the dung-heap. The door of the tavern banged shut.

The man wasn't making a sound. Was he hurt? Was he dead? If anyone came looking for him they might find me! It might be better to run away while I could. But . . . might he not have a *kopeck* or two in his pockets?

I crept across the yard and knelt beside him. There he lay, a big fellow, tall as a pine tree, flat on his back. His shirt was of heavy linen, and he wore thick well-greased boots. He had a shaggy head of hair and a long wispy beard. Just as my hand slipped into his breeches pocket, he gave a great snort and opened his eyes. His hand clamped around my wrist.

"What are you doing?" he muttered. Then he sat up and stared at me.

Was he young? Was he old? I couldn't tell. And I had never seen eyes like his — light blue-grey, they seemed to look right through me, even in the half light. I sat frozen, like a rabbit before a weasel.

"I said, 'What are you doing?' " he growled.

"N-nothing, Your Honor," I stammered. "I only wondered if you were hurt!"

He grunted. "Hoped I was, you mean, so you could

clean out my pockets, you thieving lad!" Slowly he brought a forefinger toward the end of my nose, my eyes following it until they crossed. Then he guffawed, "Why, it's not a lad at all. It's a little maid, isn't it?"

"Yes, *gospodin.*" My eyes uncrossed. If he would just let go for a moment, I'd be off. He'd never be able to catch me. But his grasp tightened.

I let fat tears well up in my eyes and slide down my cheeks. "Let me go, gospodin," I blubbered. "I'll never try to steal again. I never have before."

"Stop crying! I hate women to cry." He swung his head back and forth like a bear being baited by dogs. "Listen," he said. "My head feels like a barrel of bees. I must sleep now. You stay. Yes?" With a grunt he fell on his back and began to snore. But he still gripped my wrist.

Hour after hour I waited. My legs grew cramped, and I was hungry, and wet with dew.

He roused at dawn, and sat up, holding his head with his free hand. "Oh, Lord," he muttered. He stumbled to his feet, dragging me up with him. "It's the thieving maid," he said, staring down at me. "Scarcely bigger than a flea!" Then, "How about breakfast, flea?"

My mouth watered, but I shook my head. "Oh, no thank you, gospodin," I said. "My old grandmother needs me, and I must be getting along to her."

He snorted. "Your old grandmother, eh? The one who lets you spend your nights behind taverns?" Then suddenly he strode off, dragging me after him.

"What village do you come from?" he asked, glowering down at me. "And no more lies!"

"I . . . I don't know," I gasped, trying to keep up with him.

He gave me a burning glance.

"I *don't!*" For the place I came from was no more than a huddle of rough isbas beside a dusty path, and behind them a few hardscrabble fields hacked from the flanks of the forest.

"Your name, then, flea!"

"D-Dunia, gospodin. Dunia Ivanovna."

"Dunia Ivanovna *what?*"

I had no last name. No one I knew did. My father was Big Ivan, and another man of the same name was Little Ivan. That was all. So, "I don't know," I muttered.

He stopped and glared down at me. "You don't know much, do you?"

I tried to think of something I did know. "Mushrooms," I said.

"Mushrooms? What could such a very small flea know about mushrooms?"

"Folk say every snipe is great in his own swamp, gospodin," I told him. "Anyone who lives near the forest knows all about mushrooms."

He cocked his head. "And you've been eating many mushrooms lately, yes?"

"Yes," I said. "And berries and nuts, and wood apples . . . "

He grunted. "A runaway. I thought as much. And how long have you been in the woods?"

"Five days," I admitted.

His shaggy eyebrows shot up. "Five *days*? And the wolves haven't eaten you?"

I shook my head. "No, though one night I saw wolf eyes all around, like little green lamps."

He gave a low whistle. "And weren't you afraid?"

"Yes," I replied. "But I said my prayers, and they didn't eat me."

"God must be leading you, then," he muttered. "But why has He led you here?"

How could I answer that? I said nothing as we went on. Then, "What's *your* name, gospodin?" I ventured.

"Grigory," he replied. "Grigory Efimovich Rasputin."

We came to a very large isba. Grigory brushed straw off his shirt, then he opened the door.

"Praskovaya, my honey bee," he called.

"Grigory?" A woman in a crisp white apron appeared. She was tall and buxom, with golden braids wrapped like a crown around her head. "Where have you been?" she demanded.

"At Pyotr's tavern," he confessed. "Or, more recently, *behind* Pyotr's tavern."

Praskovaya sniffed. "On the dung-heap, by the smell of you! I suppose you cheated at cards, and they caught you! When will you ever learn? And you a man of God, Grigory — " She broke off as her eye fell on me. "Whose child is this?"

"She found me on the dung-heap," said Grigory "She survived five days in the forest, with wolves all

9

around her. God must have a special purpose for her, to have spared her like that."

Praskovaya frowned, and suddenly his expression changed.

He drew himself up and pointed his finger at her. "How dare we refuse to help her," he thundered. "We to whom God has given so much?"

Praskovaya turned pale, and took a step backward. "Yes, Grigory," she murmured.

"That's better," he said. Then, "See how timid and shy the child is."

"Sly, not shy," Praskovaya shot back. "Eyes dark as sloes, and hair to match."

Grigory gave her two smacking kisses, one on each cheek. "Not everyone can be a golden beauty like you, my flower. Say you'll at least give the child breakfast."

She blushed at his compliment. "Come along, then, child," she said, holding out her hand.

My head was itchy, so I gave it a good scratch. Praskovaya's eyes widened. She peered at my scalp, then took a step backward. "She's alive with lice!" she shrieked. "Not in my house, Grigory. Not even for our dear Lord's sake!"

"But Praskovaya — "

"Out! Take her around the back this minute!"

The door slammed behind us. "Women," he sighed. "So much fuss about a few little bugs."

Around the house, the back door opened and a metal tub was tossed out, landing on the ground with a hollow clang. A few minutes later a grim-faced woman appeared, carrying two kettles of steaming water. Praskovaya followed with two more. "Go away, Grigory," she ordered.

"As you say, my flower," he muttered, making for the door.

I took to my heels, but Praskovaya caught me. Between them the two women pulled off my clothes and dumped me into the tub. The water was scalding hot, and I shrieked in pain and fear. They were going to boil me alive and eat me! They were witches, just like Baba Yaga!

I screamed, I kicked, I fought, but the woman held me down, while Praskovaya poured lamp oil over my head. Now they were going to burn me up! I screamed louder. A cake of lye soap appeared in front of me, and I bit the hand that held it. I received a stinging slap.

"Stop it, you little savage!" Praskovaya hissed. "Bathed you will be!"

It would be my first and last bath, I promised myself.

Praskovaya dragged me out of the tub, bright red and snivelling. Wrapping me in a coarse towel, she shoved me toward the door. "Sit at the table and behave," she ordered.

Stripped as I was, I had to obey. The kitchen was a large, dark-beamed room with a huge red brick stove and a long pine table with benches beside it. A little girl with thick braids was eating a bowl of kasha. A pot of honey stood next to her bowl. "My name is Varvara," the girl announced, spooning honey over her kasha. "Who are *you?*" She licked the spoon and put it back in the pot.

"Ludmilla, give the child a bowl of the kasha," Praskovaya told the other woman. "I'll find her some old clothes. And burn those rags of hers before we are all infested!"

I wolfed down the kasha, which tasted better than anything I could remember.

Praskovaya reappeared with an armful of clothing. "Here," she said, tweaking away the towel so that I stood before them quite bare. "Try these for size."

I struggled into a pair of knickers, a vest and a petticoat. A skirt came next, and a blouse with a bit of embroidery around the neck. Never had I had anything so fine. There was even a pair of felt shoes. I had never worn shoes before. I wished my mother could see my new clothes. She'd always loved pretty things, and never had many.

Praskovaya scooped me up and set me in a chair. "Now for your hair," she said grimly. She set to work on me with a fine-toothed comb. It was worse than the bath. Far worse. Five days in the forest had turned my hair into a tangle of burrs and bits of bark.

"Ow!" I shrieked, as the comb dug into my scalp.

"Of course it hurts, you silly girl. Sit still," said Praskovaya, dragging away with the comb. "Ludmilla," she added, "come and hold her."

Tears streamed down my cheeks. I screamed and struggled until Praskovaya's patience wore thin. "It's no use," she said, putting down the comb. "It'll have to be the other."

At first I didn't understand. Then I saw the glint of scissors, and heard a snip. A great tuft of hair tumbled into my lap. "Noooo!" I wailed, clapping my hands over my hair.

"It's terribly matted. It must all come off, child," said Praskovaya.

Off it came, snip after terrible snip. At last Praskovaya put the scissors away. I reached up and felt my head. Nothing but bristles — she had cropped me to the scalp. I howled.

"Are you murdering the child?" asked Grigory, appearing in the doorway.

Praskovaya shrugged. "I had to cut her hair off. It's for her own good."

I bawled louder.

"Stop that!" snapped Grigory. "Your hair will grow back."

"But it will take *years*," I blubbered.

"Vanity is a sin before God!" he thundered.

I wiped my nose and glared down at my feet in their new shoes. This is all *your* fault, I thought.

2

A Miracle

August, 1911

"Now what?" Praskovaya demanded the next morning. "You asked me to give the child breakfast. Well, she had three square meals yesterday, and a bath and fresh clothing too. Not to mention a night in a clean bed. How much more do you expect of me?"

Grigory stroked his beard and said nothing.

Praskovaya wagged her finger at him. "She can't stay here. I've the children and the farm to see to — and you off in Petersburg half the year."

I caught my breath. Did Grigory really live in St. Petersburg, the city of the mighty tsar?

"Send her home," Praskovaya went on. "Her poor mother must be crying her eyes out."

"She's not!" I said, shaking my head. "My mother is dead."

"And your father too?" asked Grigory.

"No. But . . . " I didn't want to say that he cared for me less than for his wolfhound.

"You see?" crowed Praskovaya. "She's a wicked runaway."

Grigory sat down on a bench. "Come here, flea," he said. I went to stand before him. "Do you know the way back home?"

I stared down at my shoes. "No," I lied.

"Look at me, Dunia!" he commanded. When I obeyed, he gazed into my eyes, and I couldn't look away again. I felt as if I were falling into a well of clear water.

"Do you want to go home?" he asked.

I shook my head.

"Why? The truth, now!"

"My stepmother makes me do all the hard work. My father takes his stick to me. I'm always hungry," I said.

Grigory got to his feet and began pacing up and down the room. "God *must* be leading her," he muttered. "She escaped the wolves, and came straight to me. What is His purpose? Is it a sign?" He seemed to be getting more and more excited.

"Now, Grigory — " Praskovaya began.

"Silence, woman!" he roared. "Let me think!" Then, "A child of the people," he said to himself. "Like a gift from God. Somehow I must be meant to use her." He stopped in his tracks and stared down at me, his strange eyes widening. "Matushka," he said softly.

Whose mother was he talking about?

He turned abruptly and spoke to Praskovaya. "God must be telling me I've been away from Petersburg

15

too long, that I must return to do His work. Those in the highest places need me. Somehow this child is part of it. I must leave as soon as I can."

"That makes no sense, Grigory," Praskovaya cried. "You can't go yet! There's still most of the harvest to get in! And if you think you can leave the child here — "

Grigory cut her off with a sweep of his hand. "I'm taking her with me to Petersburg."

My heart began to pound. My clever feet had carried me into a fairy tale. I was going to St. Petersburg!

Praskovaya folded her arms and tapped one foot on the floor. "And just how am I supposed to manage the harvest without you, Grigory?" she demanded.

"I'll speak to our neighbour this afternoon. He and those lumbering sons of his are always looking for work." He put his arm around her plump shoulders. "Your harvest will still be in before anyone else's. Then you'll sit safe and snug all winter." He turned to me. "Come, my flea," he said. "I must buy a horse and *tarantass*. My wife cannot spare any of ours in the harvest season."

"Buy a cart? Why not take the river steamer to Tiumen?" Praskovaya asked.

Grigory shook his head. "Too many days to wait. And the way across the steppe is shorter."

Well, even I had seen better tarantasses than the one in the Pokrovskoe livery stable. The basketwork body of the cart had great holes in it, and one of the wheels sat askew on its axle.

Grigory gave it a kick. "How can you ask good money for this wreck, Ilya?" he demanded.

The man scratched his nose. "I'll fix the wheel, and I'll throw in some straw to block up the holes."

Grigory pulled out a wad of rubles. Ilya's eyes lit up. "You'll need a horse, Grigory Efimovich," he said eagerly. "A fine strong horse.

Grigory's eyes narrowed. "Let me see this horse," he growled.

The horse had a sway back, and its ribs showed through its mangy hide. I stroked its nose, and it pushed its bristly muzzle into my hand

Grigory walked around it, then he peered at its teeth. "I suppose you're going to tell me this sorry beast once belonged to the tsar?" he said, turning to Ilya.

Ilya snorted. "No, Grigory. I won't tell you that. But he'll get you to Tiumen all right."

Sighing, Grigory counted out more rubles, while Ilya slipped a rope halter over the horse's nose. I took the rope. "We'll be good to you, poor horse," I told it. "What's his name?" I asked.

"Who'd bother giving the beast a name?" said Ilya, stuffing the money into his pocket.

"Can I name him?" I begged Grigory.

He shrugged. "Go ahead. But don't get fond of him. I'll be selling him in Tiumen."

I thought about the noble steeds in stories, with names like Sultan, Prince and Silkmane. I could see that they wouldn't do. Then as I led the horse across the stable, he seized a turnip from a basket and crunched it between his yellow teeth.

"Hi! Stop that!" yelled Ilya, giving the horse a smack on the flank.

"*You* stop it!" I shouted, slapping his leg. "The poor thing is hungry!"

"Greedy's more like it," muttered Ilya. "He's stuffed full of my best oat hay."

"Maybe he just likes turnips," I said. Then it came to me. "Turnip! That's a good name for him."

A rider came dashing up the street, whipping his horse with a bit of rope. "Grigory Efimovich!" he bellowed as soon as he saw us. "One of your horses has been slashed with a scythe. It's bleeding to death where it lies!"

"What?" roared Grigory. Seizing the halter, he vaulted onto Turnip's back. "Have that cart ready soon," he shouted to Ilya, "or I'll cut off your ears!"

Scooping me up in front of him, he kicked Turnip into a clumsy gallop. The other rider wheeled his horse and we rode after him as if Baba Yaga herself were on our heels.

We tore up the main street, and down a narrow lane, scattering geese and ducks before us. We came out into a field where people were gathered. There was a wagon, with one horse still hitched to it. The leather traces of the second horse had been cut, and it lay stretched upon the ground. A long-handled scythe with a wicked blade lay on the stubble nearby.

Grigory sprang from Turnip's back and pushed his way through the crowd. I squirmed through after him. The air was heavy with the smell of the cut grain, and the heat of the sun beat down on my head, making me dizzy.

He knelt by the horse. Blood was pumping from a deep gash on its leg.

"The poor brute is bleeding to death," a man muttered. "Send for a gun, Grigory."

"Quiet!" hissed someone else.

Grigory knelt with his head bowed. He put his left hand over the wound and pinched the gaping edges together, crossing himself with his right hand. Blood spurted between his fingers, staining the sleeve of his shirt. He raised his eyes to the sky, and his lips moved. His face became pasty-white, and great drops of sweat beaded his forehead.

A murmur ran through the crowd, and people crossed themselves. I tore my eyes away from Grigory's face and looked down at the wound. The blood had stopped spurting! Still he held the wound closed. Then, at last, his head drooped, and his bloodstained hand slid away. I caught my breath, expecting another gush of blood, but nothing happened.

"He has stilled the blood," I heard a man mutter behind me.

"He has the gift," another agreed. "He's always had it. He is a holy man, a *starets*."

"God be praised, it's a miracle," a woman cried. Once again, people crossed themselves.

The horse lifted its head. A moment later, it got its legs under it and stumbled to its feet. A great sigh rose up from the crowd. They had all seen something that would keep their tongues busy through the long winter to come.

Grigory pulled out his pocket knife. Cutting a piece of linen from the tail of his shirt, he bound up the wound on the horse's leg. Then he picked up the cut end of the leather traces and led the animal toward Pokrovskoe. It limped badly, but no blood seeped through the bandage. The crowd parted in front of Grigory, and I trailed after him, leading Turnip.

"Run, Misha! Tell his wife," I heard a woman in the crowd say, and a small boy raced on ahead of Grigory as he plodded across the field.

When we reached the isba, Praskovaya was waiting outside. Her eyes went to Grigory's face, which was still ashen pale, then to the bandage on the horse's leg. Taking his arm, she said, as if talking to a child, "Inside. Eat. Then sleep."

Ludmilla fussed around Grigory with a basin of hot water. He dabbled his fingers in it, then rubbed them on the clean towel, leaving it soiled with blood and dirt. Kicking a bench out of his way, he flung himself down at the table and helped himself to the fragrant fish soup, plunging both hands into the tureen and pulling out the best bits. When he had eaten his fill, he heaved himself to his feet and lumbered off to the next room. The rest of us finished the soup to the sound of snoring.

3

Journey

September, 1911

The road to Tiumen wound through birch woods where golden leaves were falling.

"Is it woods all the way to Tiumen, then?" I asked.

"No, there's the steppe . . . " Grigory paused, listening. Someone was singing up ahead.

In a few minutes, we came up with a young peasant woman carrying a large basket. "Good morning, fair one," Grigory called, slowing Turnip to a walk. "Where are you off to?"

"To the other side of the forest, gospodin," she said, giving him a sideways glance.

Grigory stopped the cart and got down. He lifted the basket from her arm and said, "A pretty creature like you shouldn't carry such a load. Won't you ride with us a way?"

She grinned at him, showing dimples in both cheeks, and scrambled into the cart.

Grigory had seemed gloomy when we set out, but

now he chatted cheerfully with the woman as we went along. Soon we stopped by a stream to eat lunch. Grigory and the woman sat in the cart chewing hunks of sausage, and laughing like old friends. I unhitched Turnip and led him down to the stream.

When I got back, Grigory climbed out. "Can you drive a horse, my flea?" he asked, as he hitched Turnip.

"I don't know," I said.

"Try it," he said, and the next moment I found Turnip's reins in my hands. "He'll keep going until you pull on the reins," Grigory explained, as he clambered into the back of the tarantass.

At first I clung to the reins for dear life. But nothing went wrong, so I began to tell myself a tale about a princess driving a golden carriage. Pretty soon I heard the straw rustling, and giggles. Embarrassed, I kept my eyes on the road. Grigory was supposed to be a holy man!

Awhile later, Grigory climbed back onto the seat and sat whistling a tune through his teeth. At the edge of the wood he turned and called out, "Is this where you want to get down, fair one?"

"Yes, gospodin," she replied, pointing. "There's the path that leads to my village."

I pulled on the reins. To my delight, Turnip stopped at once.

Grigory helped the woman down and handed her the basket. "Good day to you then," he said.

She dimpled, and smoothed down her petticoats. "Good day to *you*, gospodin."

We drove out of the wood. Before us, the earth was cloaked with shimmering grass. Over it all curved a great blue bowl of sky, cloudless and bright.

"Is *this* the steppe?" I asked.

"It is, my flea."

"But it's so empty. Anybody at all could see you for miles and miles!"

"That's the beauty of it. See how blue the sky is. The sky of the steppe is the eye of God."

I squirmed. God might be looking down at me through that great blue eye. Out here He could see my running away and telling lies, when He might not have noticed them before.

We journeyed with the sun on our faces. Of people there was no sign — not a village, not a wisp of smoke. At last the great golden ball of the sun hung above the horizon.

"Where will we sleep?" I asked.

"Why, here on the steppe. Where else?" Grigory turned off the track. He hobbled Turnip and turned him loose to graze. The two of us ate our supper cold. Afterward, I rolled myself up in a blanket, but sleep wouldn't come. At last, I sat up. "What are you doing?" I asked Grigory.

"Watching the stars. Do you know the story of how the stars got into the sky?"

He knew stories! "Oh, yes!" I said. "Do you know the one about the flying ship? And the one about the bright falcon, and — "

"Suppose you tell me a story, then I'll tell you one," he said.

I settled myself cross-legged and folded my hands in my lap, for my mother had taught me that was the way to start a story. "A storyteller's hands are like birds," she would say. "They must fly into the air to help tell the story. So they must be quiet in their nest at the beginning."

"Once, long ago," I began, "there lived a beautiful girl named Vasilissa the Fair . . . "

When I finished, Grigory nodded. "Good, good. Would you like to hear the one about the firebird, the prince and the apples of gold?"

I nodded, for I never can decide which is better, listening to stories or telling them.

"Close your eyes, then," he said.

I took a last look at the vast sky spangled with thousands of stars. Just in case one of them decided to fall on me, I crept under the wagon. The story was long, and Grigory's voice somehow turned into my mother's, and I saw her face, framed by her shiny black braids, bending over me.

We spent another day and night on the steppe. Then, late in the afternoon of the third day, I heard a long, shivery wail. It sounded like a *djinn* from a fairy tale. "What's that?" I cried, clutching Grigory's arm.

"That, my flea, is the train," he replied.

"What's a train?"

"You'll soon find out."

Tiumen was much bigger than Pokrovskoe. The buildings were made of brick, not logs, and the streets were packed with people, shouting and jostling each other and plunging under the very feet of the horses. Now and then came the awful wail of the train.

"What's wrong, what's happening?" I screamed over the din.

"Nothing!" Grigory bellowed. "This is just the way it is in Tiumen." Glancing at the sun, he turned into a side street. "The Petersburg train leaves at six o'clock," he said. "There's barely enough time to sell this wretched horse and cart and buy our tickets."

Sell Turnip! I'd forgotten that was going to happen. "Couldn't he just stay in the stable here until you come back?" I asked. "He's such a good horse. He's done his best."

Grigory snorted. "Leave him eating his head off for six months? I'm not made of money!" A few moments later, he stopped before a rundown stable. "Now we'll see how little they'll give me for this nag," he muttered. Jumping down, he stomped inside.

I got down too. "It's no use, little brother," I told Turnip, stroking his nose. "He's going to sell you. May God be with you." I shook my finger at him. "And don't steal any more turnips."

In a few moments, Grigory emerged, licking his thumb and counting more rubles. He seized me by the arm, and strode off. "Hurry," he urged. "We must buy our tickets."

I trotted to keep up with him, the basket banging against my leg. We reached a broad street where a horde of people were pushing and shoving, all trying to force their way into a big building ahead of us. The train wailed, very close. This must be its home.

Grigory pulled a heavy gold cross on a chain out of his pocket and put it over his head. The cross hung gleaming on his chest as he elbowed his way through the crowd. A stout woman turned, her lips pursed to utter angry words, but when she saw Grigory's cross she stepped aside.

"Bless you, little mother," said Grigory, making the sign of the cross over her.

It was the same with the rest of the people. Their eyes went to the cross, and a murmur ran before us. "It's a starets, a holy man!" We soon reached a window with a man behind it.

"Two third-class tickets for Petersburg, my son," said Grigory, pulling rubles out of his wallet.

"Hurry, Father," the man replied. "The Petersburg train is at the platform."

Grigory dragged me through the building, and there was the train. A monster of shiny black metal, it huffed and panted, blowing steam out of the top of its head and out around its huge round feet, which rested on two rails of shiny metal. Behind it stretched a long tail of carriages stuffed with people. It was as if the train had eaten them, every one.

Grigory hustled me down the platform and boosted me into a carriage. I stumbled forward, tripping over wooden benches lined up on the floor. I dodged a crate of chickens an old babushka was wrestling with, and was butted from behind by a nanny goat. "If I had a stick, I'd give you news, little sister," I told the nanny, rubbing my backside.

Grigory scooped me up. Carrying me over his arm

like a towel, he dumped me on one of the benches, and set the basket beside me. "Keep a place for me," he commanded.

It wasn't easy. A burly *mouzhik* shepherded his large family onto two whole benches, then plopped down himself, pushing me to the floor. "Who are you to be seated, little brat, when your elders and betters can't find a place?" he muttered.

"It's not for me, gospodin," I protested. "The seat is for a holy starets on his way to Moscow."

"Starets, eh? Where is this starets?" he demanded, glancing around suspiciously.

"Here he is!" I cried, as Grigory came up behind him.

The cross did its work. "Forgive me, Father," said the peasant, jumping up. "I didn't know the seat was yours." Then, "Off with you, Masha," he added, pushing a daughter off the bench.

"Thank you, my son," said Grigory, seating himself. "I'm taking this poor orphan, a saintly child, to Petersburg." He pulled me down beside him.

Orphan? Saintly child? Grigory's smile was as smooth as cream.

The train gave a great lurch and several passengers slid to the floor. I looked out the window and saw the platform slowly sliding away behind us. My stomach gave a queer flop, and suddenly I wanted to jump out. I sneaked a glance at Grigory. What did I really know of him, after all? Except that he was sly — sly enough to walk on raw eggs without breaking them. What was he planning to do with me in St. Petersburg? But it was too late to change my mind now, for the train was going faster and swaying from side to side, its wheels clacking along the tracks.

You'd better be right, I told my feet, snug in their new shoes. I crossed myself and thought about my mother in heaven. If God was watching me, maybe she was too. I felt comforted.

Grigory and the mouzhik got more and more friendly. When people began to unpack their food baskets, the mouzhik muttered something to his wife, who handed over two chicken legs. After people had eaten, the benches were pushed against the walls, and the children were bedded down on the floor in quilts. A man pulled out a *balalaika* and began to strum, then another sang. Grigory pulled a flask out of his pocket and took a gulp. He passed it over to the mouzhik, who swigged and passed it back. I sniffed. Vodka. I noticed Grigory had taken his cross off again.

After awhile I curled up spoon-fashion between two of the mouzhik's daughters, red-cheeked little girls with wheaten braids. They snuggled against me like warm puppies, and we slept.

I woke at dawn, and leaned out the window. The land was still flat and golden. On and on we went, for more days and nights. It was hot and smelly in the carriage, and children cried and fought with each other. The grownups didn't sing or play the balalaika anymore. They just stared into space.

We passed through low mountains, and then rolled on over flatter land again. "Will we *ever* get to St. Petersburg?" I asked Grigory, who was playing cards.

"This very night, God willing," he replied.

As darkness fell, I could see a strange glow in the sky ahead of us. People began to get ready. Men smoothed their hair, and women retied their kerchiefs. The sky grew brighter, and now there were lines of lights along the tracks, leading the train into the city. I could see a gigantic building looming before us, and pulled my head in, suddenly afraid. At last, with a screech, the train stopped.

The mouzhik embraced Grigory. "Go on with the Lord's work, little Father," he said, winking.

Grigory, very much the starets again, made the sign of the cross over him. "Farewell, my son. And may the Lord bless you and yours," he said.

People swarmed like ants on the platform. I clung tightly to Grigory's coat as he made his way outside, where a line of carriages waited. He lifted me into one. "Fifty-four Gorokhovaya Ulitsa," he told the driver.

I ran my hand over the shiny leather of the seat. "It's very grand," I whispered.

Grigory laughed. "This rattletrap of a *droshky?*"

I stared all around me as the carriage threaded through the crowded streets. They were lit as bright as day by huge lamps stuck on the top of poles. There were palaces even bigger than the ones in my dreams, and carriages, and throngs of richly-dressed people. We drove down a broad avenue, then turned into a narrower street.

"Here we are," said Grigory. He paid the driver while I scrambled out with the basket.

The building was built around a courtyard with a curly iron gate. A doorkeeper greeted Grigory, rubbing his hands together and bowing respectfully. "Welcome back, Grigory Efimovich. Now we'll have lineups at the door again."

"Yes, Nikolai, and you'll be getting fat tips again for helping people jump the queue," said Grigory, clapping him on the shoulder. "Is it not so, little brother?"

Nikolai ducked his head, grinning. "It is so, gospodin. But where the lion dines may not the jackal gnaw the scraps?"

Grigory laughed. Turning toward the stairs, he said, "Is my Marochka here?"

"Yes, Grigory Efimovich. Though probably asleep by now."

We climbed two flights of stairs, then Grigory took out a key and opened a door. He pressed something on the wall, and suddenly the room was filled with bright light. I gasped and took a step backward. "Electric lights," he explained. "A wonder of God."

We were in a large room, with furniture and curtains made of rich red material. A door opened and a stout woman in a long robe appeared. "Grigory Efimovich!" she exclaimed. "Is the harvest over so soon?"

"Praskovaya is seeing to it, Katya. It was time for me to return."

Katya turned her gaze on me. "Who's this?" she asked.

"Nobody at all, really," said Grigory. "A kind of flea I've picked up in my travels."

She frowned. "The last street waif you brought here stole a silver spoon."

"Nay," said Grigory. "I was only joking. This is Dunia, and she's from . . . Well, from Pokrovskoe as near as not. Just look how neat and clean she is. Praskovaya has seen to that."

Katya untied my kerchief, and her eyes widened at the sight of my shorn head. "I see how Praskovaya has had to manage," she said. "The child was louse-ridden, am I right?"

"Well, she's not now," said Grigory. "I leave her to you. I must pray and then rest."

Katya sighed. "Come along, then. You must have a bath," she said. "You've probably picked up more bugs on that filthy train."

Another bath! But I was too tired to fight. Katya didn't find any bugs, so she just washed me with sweet-smelling soap and bundled me into a too-big nightgown. She gave me bread and milk and tucked me into bed. I buried my nose in the clean linen pillow and tumbled into sleep.

4

Wonders

September, 1911

I woke to the sound of voices. The door was ajar, so I stole over and put my eye to the crack.

Grigory was slouched in an armchair. A golden-haired girl was leaning against his shoulder, stroking his hair. Katya was there too.

"You can't keep Dunia here," Katya was saying. "It's not fair to Marochka. You don't want to make your own daughter jealous."

"Dunia won't be staying here!" snapped Grigory. He was dressed in fine clothes and shiny boots, and he was wearing his cross. "I'm going to use her to open the hearts of Batushka and Matushka."

Whose father and mother did he mean? I wondered.

Katya's hand flew to her mouth. "The Batushka Tsar? The Tsarina? You shouldn't meddle with grand folk, Grigory. You'll get into trouble!"

He rubbed his hands. "Nonsense! They need me to guide them. And this child can help."

I pushed the door a crack wider open. "Papa, look!" cried Marochka, pointing.

"Eavesdropping!" Katya sailed over, grabbed my ear, and dragged me into the room.

"Ow!" I cried, trying to get away. "No, I wasn't — "

"Of course you were," said Grigory. "Let her go," he ordered.

I backed away, rubbing my ear, and let tears well up and trickle down my cheeks.

"Don't blubber," snarled Grigory. Turning to Katya, he said, "She'll need things — underclothes, night-gowns . . . All good, all plain. Buy them now, today."

"But, Grigory Efimovich — "

"No buts!" he roared. "I'm going out. When I get back I want it done, do you hear me?" The door slammed behind him.

Katya brushed and ironed my clothes, muttering under her breath all the while. When I was dressed, we went downstairs and she hailed a passing droshky. Soon we were riding down a grand street lined on both sides with huge buildings made of honey-coloured stone.

"Are they all palaces?" I was expecting a prince or princess with a golden crown any minute.

"People don't live here," said Katya. "These are government buildings."

We turned off the great avenue. The streets were narrower now, and echoed with the cries of vendors selling everything from sausages to flowers. Swarms of beggars ran after us calling out for money. Knots of angry-looking men in rough clothing were gathered on street corners, holding banners. Outside many shops, long lines of women and old people waited.

"Why aren't the men at work?" I asked.

Katya pursed her lips and frowned. "They are on strike against the government."

"What is the government?"

"Why, the Tsar and his ministers. The workers want more freedom for the people."

"And the women?" I asked. "Why do they wait?

"For bread and meat," said Katya. "God give them patience. They may wait all day and then find there is nothing left in the shops."

I didn't understand. In our village all the men worked, and nobody knew anything about a government. And we all knew if there was food or not. If not, we went hungry.

The droshky stopped before a grand stone building. People were coming out with packages and bundles, so I thought it must be a store, though it looked like a palace.

"Hold tightly to my hand," warned Katya.

There was so much to see that my eyes nearly bulged out of my head with looking. The warm air made me dizzy. Up and up we climbed, one set of shiny stone stairs after another, until we reached the right floor. Katya bought me underwear and nightgowns, plain and thick. After that, a pair of ugly black shoes that made my feet feel like stones.

Back at Grigory's apartment, a line of people stretched across the courtyard and all the way up the stairs. Some were poorly dressed, but many wore furs and shiny silks. Nikolai was keeping them in order. A woman pressed something into his hand, and at once he showed her to a place farther up the stairs. The others grumbled and protested, but Nikolai frowned at them, and they fell silent.

"Are they waiting for bread and meat?" I asked Katya.

"They are waiting for Grigory Efimovich. But how do they knew he's back?"

What could all these people want with Grigory? Soon afterward, we heard a babble of voices outside the apartment. The door opened, and Grigory appeared. "Yes, yes, I will see you all," he said as he came in.

Marochka followed him in with her schoolbag. "Come," Katya said to her. "We'll go to my room while your father sees people. You too, Dunia."

A murmur of voices came from behind the door. Katya lay back in her armchair, and put a handkerchief over her face. Soon we heard faint snores.

Marochka put her ear against the door. Then she shrugged. "It's boring today," she said.

"But what does he say to them?" I wanted to know.

"Papa cures people's ills and helps them solve their problems," she said. "He's famous!"

"Does he get money for doing it?" I asked.

"Ye-sss . . . " she admitted. "But he gives most of it away. He just keeps enough to pay for my school expenses. And for Katya and the apartment."

"Doesn't he send any money to your mother in Pokrovskoe, then?"

"Well, of course he does."

I thought for a moment. "Why doesn't your whole family live here in St. Petersburg, anyway?"

"You *are* nosy!" Marochka snapped. "My mother doesn't like the city. She likes the farm, and so does my brother, Pyotr. Mama will send Varvara here to go to school, though, as soon as she's old enough."

There was a harsh jangling sound in the other room. It sounded twice, three times, and then I heard Grigory's voice saying loudly, *"Da?* Yes, this is Grigory. I'm busy now. Call me later."

"What was that?" I asked Marochka.

"The telephone, stupid. Don't you know what a telephone is?"

Well, I didn't, but I wouldn't let *her* know. It must be a magical way for people to talk to each other. Another wonder of God, like the electric lights.

A church bell sounded five o'clock, and Katya woke up with a snort. "Why didn't you wake me, Marochka?" she said, bustling into the kitchen. "It's past tea time. Let your father know." Then, as Marochka jumped up, she added, "No, don't go in. Just knock twice on the door. Dunia, help me make the tea."

Soon Grigory appeared, yawning and stretching as if he'd been hard at work.

Katya handed him a glass of tea with many spoonfuls of sugar. He wolfed down a huge plateful of potatoes, sauerkraut and black bread, washing it all down with great gulps of tea. After several more glassfuls, he stood up, wiping his hands on his beard. "Come with me, Dunia," he said. He sat down in his big arm-chair in the other room, and made me stand in front of him. "Now," he said. "Have you thought about why so many strange things have happened to you?"

Of course I had. I was in a fairy tale.

"It's no accident that you found me on that dung-heap, you know," he went on. "God doesn't work by accident. I believe He led you there to meet me."

I'd thought it was my own clever feet. "God *meant* me to run away?"

"He led you every step, my flea." Grigory's pale eyes gleamed, and he fingered his gold cross. "Who else put food into your mouth? Kept you safe when there were wolves all around you?"

"But why did He do it?"

"Ah!" Grigory held up a forefinger. "God led you to me, Dunia, to help me save Russia." He held my eyes with his. I tried to look away from those blue-grey pools, but I couldn't. His voice seemed to be coming from very far away, yet I could see him right there in front of me. "You must believe two things, my flea," he said in a singsong voice. "First, our beloved Russia is in danger. From enemies both inside and out."

"Russia is in danger," I repeated.

"That's right. The second thing is that our Little Father, our Batushka Tsar, is a good man, but he is led this way and that way by bad advisors. He needs God's help. My help."

It didn't make sense, I thought dizzily. How could Grigory tell the Batushka Tsar what to do?

He seemed to sense my doubt. "It's true," he insisted. "I am sent by God to guide the Tsar. You *must* believe this, Dunia, and help me do God's work."

"What do you want me to do?" I mumbled.

He leaned back, smiling. "There is a lady. Her name is Ania. Ania Vyrubova. She's a very good friend of Matushka, our Little Mother, the Tsarina. Ania knows that I can help Batushka and Matushka see things right. She has a little house near the Tsar's palace at Tsarskoe Selo, and now and then I meet Batushka and Matushka there."

"Don't you go to the palace?" I asked.

"Sometimes," Grigory replied. "But there are many spies and enemies there. More often Ania just brings me messages from the Tsarina, and takes her mine, or she carries messages between us."

"But you really do know the Tsar?" I asked.

"Haven't I just said so? Listen. Ania is very lonely. She needs someone to love her and keep her spirits up. Someone who can go unnoticed to the palace when she can't, or even come and go freely between Petersburg and Tsarskoe Selo. Do you understand?"

I shook my head.

"I mean *you*, Dunia," he said. "God has sent you because we need you. Who would suspect a child, after all?" He stroked his beard. "Ania is away now, but when she gets back in October you will meet her. You must try hard to please her. If you do, you will live well. You will see Batushka and Matushka sometimes, maybe the grand duchesses and the Heir too. You'd like that!"

"Yes . . . " This fairy tale was getting more and more wonderful. "But — "

"But *what?*" snapped Grigory.

"You said I have to love Ania. What if I don't?"

Grigory's eyes blazed and he stood up so suddenly that I jumped back. "Love her? Of course you'll love her!" he thundered, staring down at me. "Because I tell you to. And if you don't love her, then you'll pretend to, or it will be the worse for you!"

I was frightened. I had seen him change from starets to sinner and back again, but now it was as if a wild wolf was looking out through his eyes. Maybe he was a shape-shifter! I backed away from him. "I'll do it," I whispered.

"What?" he bellowed. "Speak up!"

"I'll do it!" I cried. Then I burst into tears, and for once they were real enough.

5

Ania

October, 1911

Ania was big and soft, like a rose about to lose its petals. She had a doll's face, with huge grey-blue eyes, pink cheeks and pouting lips. Her masses of light brown hair were piled high under a feathered hat, and her dress was covered with bows and frills and ribbons.

She looked me over. "You can't mean *this* child, Grigory!" she exclaimed.

"This is Madame Ania Alexandrovna Vyrubova," Grigory said to me. "Kiss her hand."

"Why?" I asked

Grigory chuckled. "See?" he said to Ania. "She's a real peasant."

Ania frowned. "But that awful hair — and such a bold expression."

"Her hair will grow. She has had an illness, that's all. And haven't I just finished telling you how important this is?" Grigory's voice was soft, but there was iron in it. Ania's lips quivered.

"Dunia was led to me by God himself," he went on. "She is a tool put into our hands, and we must use her. And you'll have someone of your very own at last, someone to keep you company, carry your messages . . . " He stroked his beard and added, "I thought you believed in me, Ania."

Tears sprang to Ania's eyes, "I do believe in you. Truly I do!" she cried. She seized his hand, and kissed it. "I'll take Dunia, if you want me to. I only thought that — "

Grigory squeezed her shoulder. "*Never* think, Ania. Pretty butterflies like you are meant for sweeter things." A strange expression flickered in his eyes for a moment.

She blushed and gazed up at him with adoring eyes.

Well, make yourself a sheep and the wolf is ready, I thought.

Grigory called Katya in. "Pack up Dunia's things," he ordered.

Katya made a neat bundle of my things. "Putting a child into the care of that woman!" she muttered. "Why I wouldn't trust her to take care of a cat!" Then, with a glance at me, "Now don't worry, Dunia. Madame Vyrubova lives right near the Tsar's palace. You'll love it there. Why, there are deer tame enough to eat from your hand, I hear tell, and black swans . . . "

"Well, Dunia," said Grigory. "We've come a long way from the place where we met."

The dung-heap, he meant. Suddenly I felt all shivery and wanted to cry. Grigory was strange, and sometimes he frightened me, but at least he was a peasant too. How could I please this spoiled fine lady? What if I couldn't? She'd complain to Grigory, and he'd find someone else for his plan. He might turn me out on the streets of St. Petersburg, or send me back to Pokrovskoe. And what would I do then?

"No tears," Grigory said. "You'll be seeing me sooner than you think. And you wanted to see palaces and princes and princesses, didn't you? Well, now you will." He grinned, showing all his teeth. "You must be careful what you wish for in this world, my flea. Sometimes you get it!"

A glossy carriage was waiting in the street. It had a picture of a crowned eagle with two heads painted on the side in black and gold. A small crowd had gathered. "It's the imperial coat of arms," someone said. "Has the Tsarina come to see Rasputin?"

"No, look, it's the Vyrubova. Probably carrying messages from Rasputin."

Ania ignored him and swished into the carriage, telling the driver to take us to the train station. The train we took was smaller than the one from Tiumen, but the carriage we sat in was far grander. The seats were made of some soft stuff, and had fancy lace-things on their backs.

I pressed my nose to the carriage window. St. Petersburg was even bigger than I'd thought, and most of it wasn't grand at all. I saw row after row of dreary brick houses all squashed together. Other buildings, big and square, belched thick black smoke into the sky.

The train stopped at the edge of the city. A group of men wearing rough blue overalls were on the platform waving banners. "Bread! Justice! Freedom!" they chanted. I stared at the strange black squiggles on the banners. I knew they were called words, for Marochka had showed off her writing and made fun of me because I couldn't read it. Could workmen read and write too?

"What do the banners say?" I asked Ania.

"Nothing you need to worry about. Pull the blinds down."

"Are the men on strike?"

Ania yawned. "I really couldn't say."

The train moved out of the station, and the shouts died away behind us. I rolled up the blinds again. We were out in flat swampy countryside now. "Is it far?" I asked.

"Only ten minutes' ride."

"Ten minutes! Grigory and I were on the train for three whole days. With goats and chickens."

Ania shuddered. "How horrible!" She rooted in her handbag, and pulled out a box wrapped in gold paper. Inside were round brown things. She popped one into her mouth.

"Is that medicine?"

Ania raised her eyebrows. "Have you never seen chocolates before?" she asked.

I shook my head. She held out the box, and I put one of the things in my mouth. "Oh!" I gasped, closing my eyes. When I opened them, Ania was smiling at me for the very first time.

"Good?" she asked.

"It was . . . *wickedly* good!"

"And wickedly fattening. I should know," she sighed, looking down at her ample lap.

"You're very pretty," I told her. "Where I come from, people think skinny people are ugly."

Ania brightened. "They do?"

I nodded. Had I not been told often enough by my stepmother how skinny and ugly I was?

"Do you miss your home very much, Dunia?"

"No!" I said quickly. "I didn't like it. At least, I didn't like living with my father and stepmother."

"I see." Ania's blue eyes looked cloudy. "Do you think you'll like living with *me?*"

I thought about it. She had chocolates. "I think so, Ania Alexandrovna," I said.

"I hope you will. It's important to Father Grigory. He wants you to help me."

"Carry messages?"

Ania nodded. "What else did he tell you?"

"That you're friends with the Matushka Tsarina, and that she and the Batushka Tsar are surrounded by enemies."

"That's true enough." She sighed.

"What is she like?" I asked, suddenly curious. "The Matushka?"

Ania's face lit up. "Oh, she's the most wonderful person in the world. She's so kind. But she's shy, so people say she's haughty and cold-hearted. So untrue.

People even say she is still German at heart, and doesn't love Russia. That is a lie, a black lie!"

The train began to slow down. When we drew up to the platform, a man in a uniform opened the carriage door and helped Ania down. I jumped down after her.

"Igor, this is Dunia. She's going to live with me," explained Ania.

The man raised his eyebrows.

The station had peaked wooden roofs with lacy carvings all around. A large sign hung above the platform. I tugged at Ania's sleeve. "What does that say?" I asked.

"Why, it says Tsarskoe Selo, you funny child. What else would it say?"

Tsarskoe Selo, the Tsar's Village. But why would the Tsar live in a village when he had the Winter Palace in St. Petersburg?

Igor helped Ania into a carriage. Tsarskoe Selo was certainly not like any village I had ever seen. It was a town, freshly-painted and neat, its streets thronged with well-dressed folk. We drove down a long street lined on one side with fine houses all painted the same shade of bluish green, with white-pillared porches. On the other side of the street stretched a tall iron fence with trees inside. Fierce-looking men patrolled it on horseback. They wore black fur caps and bright red uniforms. Sharp swords swung from their belts.

"Who are *they*?" I whispered, afraid one of them might hear me.

"The Cossacks," she replied. "The Tsar's special guards."

Cossacks! I shuddered. Even in my village we had heard of those wild horsemen from southern Russia. Mothers told children the Cossacks would carry them off if they were bad.

The carriage pulled up before a gate. Guards hurried to swing it open, saluting as we drove through. Beyond the woods was a huge meadow of green grass clipped as short and smooth as a carpet. In the middle of it was a large lake with a little island in it. Black swans floated on its mirror-smooth surface, and beyond, at the top of a hill, stood a blue-and-white palace with golden domes. Surely *this* was the Batushka Tsar's home at last.

The carriage swept around the lake. Right ahead of us stood a small building painted a cheerful yellow. There was a wood behind it. Beyond the wood rose the roof of a smaller white palace.

"Is this where you live?" I asked Ania.

She nodded. "The Tsarina lets me live in this cottage, so I can be close to them."

"You mean they live *there?*" I asked, pointing to the white palace. "Not in the palace of the golden domes?"

"The Catherine Palace? No. The family lives here, in the Alexander Palace."

A woman in black and white opened the front door. "Vera, this is Dunia," Ania said. "She has come to live with me."

Vera bobbed a curtsey, and her sharp little eyes raked me over.

"Put Dunia's things in the green room," Ania went on, taking off her gloves.

"Yes, *gospozha*," replied Vera with another bob.

I looked around. The big room off the hall was all fluffy and frilly, just like Ania herself. Every table and chair had a flounce or a skirt. The walls were covered with pictures and icons.

Ania sank into a chair. "Show Dunia her room," she said to Vera. "And then bring me tea."

The green room was at the back, looking into the woods. Vera dumped my bundle on the bed. "And where did she find *you*?" she asked.

"I'm . . . I'm a friend of Grigory Efimovich."

"Oh ho," she said. "That explains it. Ania Alexandrovna will do anything for Father Grigory."

The door closed behind her. My stomach growled, and I decided to look for the kitchen. I could ask for something to eat — or filch something if no one was looking.

When I reached the kitchen, I found Igor and Vera eating their afternoon meal.

"What do *you* want?" asked Vera.

"I'm hungry," I said, eyeing her plate.

Vera shrugged. "Well, *she* didn't say anything about feeding you."

"Ania Alexandrovna probably just forgot," said Igor.

"Well, sit down then," said Vera. She spooned stew onto a plate and put it before me.

I set to before she could change her mind. "It's very good," I said with my mouth full.

She shrugged, and banged a mug of milk down in front of me.

I can get around *her,* I told myself, gulping it down.

Igor tipped back his chair. "How did you meet Ania Alexandrovna?" he asked.

"She's a creature of Father Grigory's," sniffed Vera.

I bristled. "My family knows him in Pokrovskoe," I lied. Then Marochka's writing popped into my head. "He's going to find a way for me to go to school."

Igor whistled. "He must owe your family a big favour. What — "

He stopped as a little bell set over the kitchen door tinkled. "What does *she* want now?" complained Vera, getting up. Soon she returned to tell me, "She wants *you.*"

I found Ania in the room with the icons. "Are you hungry, Dunia?" she asked. "I forgot about you."

"No, Ania Alexandrovna," I said. "I ate in the kitchen."

She looked worried. "I'm not sure Father Grigory would want you to be with the servants . . . He didn't tell me exactly what to do with you, you see. So I really don't know . . . I'll telephone him."

The telephone hung in the front hall. Lifting the receiver, Ania spoke into the mouthpiece. "Switchboard?" She gave a number, and after a few moments said, "Father Grigory? It's Ania." She paused, then, "You're seeing the Tsarina tonight? Yes. Yes. I'll bring Dunia."

I was going to the palace! No fairy tale could be better than this!

6

Struggles

October, 1911

"I hope Father Grigory is here," Ania fretted as we followed the path to the palace that evening. "He said to bring you, but Alexandra Feodorovna doesn't like to meet new people."

"Who's Alexandra Feodorovna?" I asked.

"Why, the Tsarina, you ignorant child," snapped Ania.

Though much plainer than the palace of the golden domes, the Alexander Palace was still huge. We crunched across a gravel courtyard that led to a side entrance. Tall guards in gold-braided uniforms saluted as we climbed a flight of broad stairs. More men in fancy uniforms swung open the doors for us, and we stepped into a wide hall.

It was like a forest made of gold and shiny stone. Tall pillars rose toward the ceiling all around, and right over us hung a glittering glass thing with lights, like a waterfall frozen in mid-air. As we walked forward, my feet first slipped on polished wood and then sank into thick rugs. Through lofty arches ahead I glimpsed rooms beyond rooms, each one grander than the last.

"Hurry!" said Ania, hustling me along. "The Tsarina is expecting me, and she doesn't like to be kept waiting."

The last doorway was guarded by two enormous men whose hands and faces were black. Black! I'd never seen such a thing. One of them winked at me as we passed.

"How did they get that colour?" I asked, craning my neck to look back at them.

"They're from Africa. All the people there are black."

We crossed a green room, and stopped on the threshold of one the colour of lilacs. Its walls were covered in silk. Potted plants and folding screens divided it into sections. Though it was nearly winter, there were flowers everywhere! The air smelled of roses and lilies — it was like stepping back into summer.

"Where do all the flowers come from?" I gasped, sniffing.

"Shush!" hissed Ania. "The Tsarina has her favourite kinds sent every day from the South."

In the middle of the room stood a round table covered with golden icons. In one corner, a woman who looked some years older than Ania lay propped up on a lilac-coloured sofa with an embroidery hoop in her hands.

"You're late, Ania," she said. "And . . . who is this?" she added, her delicate eyebrows drawing together in a frown.

"Forgive me," babbled Ania. "I . . . I didn't mean to be late. Father Grigory told me . . . Isn't he here?"

"Sit down, Ania," said the woman. "And stop fussing. No, Father Grigory isn't here yet." Then, as Ania settled onto a chair beside her, "Now tell me what this is all about. Who is this child?"

"I hardly know how to tell you," Ania began. "It's all so strange . . . "

I hung back, feeling frightened among these great people, and wondering when the Tsarina was coming.

Suddenly a head popped out from behind one of the large potted plants. It was a girl of about my own age, with long fair hair and darker eyebrows. She stared at me, then glancing over her shoulder, she called, "Mashka, come and see. There's a Thing here!"

"What?" A slightly older girl appeared behind her.

"I'm not sure what it is," said the first girl, planting herself right in front of me. She was very short, not much taller than I was. "It *might* be a girl of some sort." She cocked her head. "But it's so odd-looking, it might not be."

I blushed.

"Nastasia, that's rude!" said the other one. She was plump, with rich brown hair and pink cheeks and the biggest dark blue eyes I had ever seen. "Are you a friend of Ania's?" she asked.

"I'm . . . I'm going to live with her," I faltered.

51

"Live with Ania?" demanded the Nastasia girl. "Who says so?"

"Grigory," I said.

"Father Grigory! Mama, did you hear that?" she called to the woman on the sofa.

"Don't bellow, Anastasia," the woman replied. "Ania has just been telling me about the girl. Though I must say, I don't know what Grigory could be thinking of." Then, "Come here, child," she added.

I went over and stood before her.

"This is Dunia," Ania explained to the woman, wringing her hands. "Oh, Alexandra Feodorovna, I hope you're not angry with me. But Grigory insisted that I bring her. He says it's important."

Alexandra Feodorovna? This was our Matushka Tsarina! But how could it be? Where were her golden crown and her robes of ermine and silk?

I dropped to my knees and stared up. Her face was pure and clear, like a saint in an icon. She must have been very beautiful once, with her red-gold hair and dark grey eyes, but she looked worn out, as if she had been suffering. She was still frowning a little, and I could see she wasn't pleased to find a stranger in her rooms. I wished I were a hundred *versts* away.

"Get up, stupid," said Anastasia. "People don't fall on their knees here!"

"Anastasia!" said the Tsarina. "We don't talk to guests that way."

The girl called Mashka drew me to my feet. "You might as well meet all of us," she said, smiling. "I'm Marie Nikolaevna, and this is my sister Anastasia."

Anastasia glowered at me, her dark brows almost drawing into one solid line.

"My older sister, Tatiana," Marie went on, nodding at a tall girl with dark auburn hair who sat over in a far corner of the room. The girl lifted her chin and looked me over gravely. "And my oldest-of-all sister, Olga." A fair-haired girl with a turned-up nose glanced up from a book and gave me a quick smile. "Now you've met OTMA," said Marie. "That's a word we made up from the first letters of our names."

"Are . . . Are you the grand duchesses?" I asked.

Anastasia rolled her eyes, and made a pair of horns with her fingers. "No," she replied. "I'm a goat. Marie, here, is a mule — she's stubborn enough. Tatiana is a deer. Olga is a wild horse."

What was she talking about? I stared at her with my mouth open.

Marie laughed. "Don't mind *her*," she said. "She's quite mad, aren't you, Nastasia?"

"Mad and *bad*," Anastasia agreed. Then she turned her back on me.

Just then, Grigory appeared. "Ah, Matushka," he boomed. "How are you? And how is the Tsarevich?" He bent over Alexandra Feodorovna and kissed her on both cheeks!

"Grigory!" The Tsarina's tired face lit up. She held out both hands to him, and he squeezed them in his huge paws. "My poor old heart pains me, but what does that matter? Because Alexei is so much better. He can bend his arm now. It is because of your prayers, I know it!"

Grigory nodded. "I told you God would listen to me." He grinned at the grand duchesses. "So," he said. "You young ladies have already met my flea, have you?"

"Your *flea?*" Anastasia guffawed, turning around.

I wished the floor would open and swallow me up.

"Well, she's as small and dark as a flea, isn't she?" said Grigory. "Why she's even smaller than you, Anastasia Nikolaevna."

Anastasia beamed. "Yes, she is, isn't she?" she agreed.

Grigory turned back to the Tsarina. "Now, Matushka, I shall explain it all to you. God has led this child to me, and for a purpose that concerns you. I know you understand that the peasants are the true soul of Russia. It is why you trust me and value my advice."

The Tsarina nodded, her eyes fixed on his.

"But I can't be with you all the time. So maybe you need to be reminded sometimes about who your real subjects are?" And here he gently shook his finger at her.

She smiled. "Ah, Grigory. How you lecture me!"

But she lets him do it! I thought, astonished.

"Dunia!" Without taking his eyes from the Tsarina's face, Grigory snapped his fingers. I went over and stood beside him. He put his hand on my shoulder and said, "Here is a true Russian soul. Why, a month ago she was living in a village in the Siberian forest, surrounded by wolves!"

"Good heavens, Grigory!" exclaimed the Tsarina, staring at me.

"I want you to have her near you," Grigory went on. "As a token of the real Russia in the midst of all this vanity." He waved his hand at her beautiful room. "Look at Dunia, listen to her talk, and you will remember what it means to be Matushka, the Little Mother of the Russian people."

The Tsarina toyed with a string of pearls that twined around her neck and fell to her waist. Her gaze was troubled. "Yes, I do see what you mean, Grigory. But I don't quite understand. You don't mean her to live with us in the palace, do you? I'm not sure the Tsar . . ."

Grigory chuckled. "Batushka will do as you tell him. Does he not always? But no, Matushka. Dunia will live with Ania."

Ania had sat listening to them, her head turning from Grigory to the Tsarina and back again, exactly like a dog waiting for scraps at the table. Now she uttered a little yelp of protest.

Grigory frowned at her. "Now, Ania. We've discussed this already, remember. You know how lonely you are in your little house when you cannot be with Matushka."

The Tsarina was smiling now. "Yes, Grigory. Ania *is* lonely sometimes, aren't you Ania?" Here she reached out and squeezed Ania's hand. "It would be good for you to have a young person about you. Think what joy my precious children are to me!"

"I'm perfectly happy as I am. Perfectly," Ania gasped, shaking her head.

She still didn't want me, I thought, worried. I hadn't pleased her enough.

"But the messages, Ania," Grigory reminded her patiently. "I need you to relay them to Matushka, yet you know how your every move is watched now because you are Matushka's friend. You cannot come and go unnoticed. Why, people even listen in when you talk to Matushka on the telephone."

"Grigory is right," said the Tsarina. "Dunia could come and go more easily than you, Ania. And when she's older she could even go to Petersburg to see Grigory. Just think of all the journeys it would save you. I know how weary you get sometimes."

Ania's full lower lip trembled, and her blue eyes filled with tears. "Yes, yes, it's true. I do get weary," she whimpered. "But . . . But . . ."

Grigory put his hands on her shoulders. "No more buts, Ania. Dunia will stay with you and do your bidding. Soon you'll wonder how you ever did without her — you'll see."

And so I began my life with Ania. Early each morning, she would send me scurrying through the autumn woods to the palace to see if the Tsarina had any messages. The Tsarina would always greet me with a smile now, though her ladies-in-waiting didn't. They frowned and tried to listen to what she told me, until she waved them away. Sometimes the Tsarina had no messages for Grigory, and just sent me away again, but often she wanted him to know how the Tsarevich had passed the night. He seemed to be sick. I didn't understand much about it, but I listened carefully so I could remember every word. I never saw the grand duchesses up close on these visits, but I glimpsed Anastasia once. She made a face and ran out of the room, banging the door behind her.

After a visit to the palace, I would run back to the cottage and repeat the Tsarina's message to Ania, and she would telephone Grigory to ask for special prayers. Some afternoons, we would both go to visit the Tsarina. Ania would tell her how Grigory was and what he had said on the telephone. Then the two of them would sew and chat. Now and then the Tsarina would ask me a question.

"What do people say about the Tsar in your village, Dunia?" she asked one day.

I thought for a moment. "They say that when the Tsar coughs, all Russia catches cold."

She laughed. "You see?" she said, turning to Ania. "Our good peasants know how important the Tsar is, even if the politicians in the Duma don't! Grigory is right — Dunia *is* a comfort."

After tea, Ania and I would go back to her cottage. Sometimes she went back to the palace in the evening, but I never did.

Nobody ever tried to stop me on these visits, not even the African guards. One of them usually stared straight ahead whenever he saw me coming. The other would give me a wink if there was no one else to see us.

One morning, fascinated by their rich satin uniforms and feathered turbans, I paused to stare at them. The slightly taller man was the one who sometimes winked at me. This time he spoke.

"What are you about, little miss?" he asked.

I understood him! "Do Africans speak Russian?" I gasped.

He jerked his thumb at his companion. "That one speaks French, too. But I'm not from Africa. I'm from the U. S. of A."

"Where's that?"

"Away across the ocean in North America. Even farther away than Africa."

"How did you get all the way here, then? And why can you speak Russian?"

He grinned. "Now, *that's* a mighty long story, and parts of it aren't for little ears. What's your name?"

"Dunia Ivanovna, gospodin."

"None of that 'your honour' stuff. I'll call you Dunia, and you can call me Jim," he said.

After that, I'd often stop to talk to him, if nobody else was around. The other guard never spoke.

"He takes his job mighty seriously," Jim explained to me once. "Now me, I come from the land of the free, and we don't hold much with this tsar business. We got rid of our own king long ago."

"Got rid of him? How?"

"Just said, 'Goodbye, King, won't be needing you anymore,'" said Jim. Then he added, " Of course, we had to whip him in some battles before he took us seriously."

I was puzzled. Tsars and kings came from God. How could you just get rid of them?

All through that autumn, Ania would make the journey to St. Petersburg twice a week, to see Grigory. One day when she returned, she said, "Father Grigory wants me to teach you to read and write, Dunia. We'll begin today."

Read and write! "I'll try hard to learn," I promised. And I did try. Ania had me copy the letters of the alphabet and lists of words. Hour after hour, day after day, I struggled, my pencil clamped between stiff fingers. But the words danced circles in my head, and I only learned to scrawl a few of them. After weeks of trying, I broke down in tears. "I can't learn it, I just can't!" I wailed.

"I knew I couldn't teach anyone!" sighed Ania.

So I went around with an ache in my heart. I'd always known I wasn't pretty, but now I knew I was stupid.

One morning on my way back from the palace, a tame deer came quite close. I dug in my pocket for a sugar lump. The deer took it and bounded away, and then, right behind me, a voice said, "Who said you could feed my deer?"

Turning around, I found myself face to face with a young boy. The sun glancing through the bare trees lit up his red-gold hair, and for a moment I wondered if he were an elven prince. But he looked just like the

Tsarina, and I realized that he must be the Tsarevich Alexei, the Heir to the Throne. Behind him stood a be-whiskered man.

"Never mind about the deer," said the Tsarevich, grinning. "You can feed them if you like. Are you the girl who lives with Ania?"

I didn't know whether to bow, curtsey or run away. This boy would be the Tsar of All the Russias some-day! I had carried many messages about him in the last weeks, but he didn't look sick, though he held one arm a bit stiffly.

"Cat got your tongue?" he asked.

"No," I said. "I just never know what to say to grand folk."

"So you know who I am!" The Tsarevich laughed, and turned to the man who was with him. "Do you think she's frightened of me, Pyotr Vassilievich?"

The whiskered fellow chuckled. "Not much. Come, young lady, walk along with us a way. It's good for the Tsarevich to see new faces. It doesn't happen very often."

I fell in beside them, scuffing through the dead leaves that carpeted the ground.

"Well, you know me. And this is my tutor, Pyotr Vassilievich Petrov," said Alexei, giving me a side-ways glance. "What's your name?"

"Dunia Ivanovna."

"I remember now," he said. "My sister Anastasia told me about you."

I scowled and gave the leaves a good kick.

"Oh ho!" crowed Alexei. "You don't like Anastasia. Did she make fun of you?"

I nodded.

"Now, don't go all glum again," he coaxed. "Listen, you mustn't mind Nastasia. She's like that with everyone. She's a *shvipsik*, a regular imp, isn't she, Pyotr Vassilievich?"

The tutor sighed, and raised his eyes to heaven. "Worse than a shvipsik sometimes."

"Marie Nikolaevna was nice to me," I ventured.

"Mashka would be," he said, nodding. "*She's* nice to everyone." He laughed. "She's so good that we say she can't be our true sister. Papa says he worries that she'll sprout angel's wings!"

They'd have to be sturdy wings to lift plump Marie Nikolaevna! I grinned at the thought.

"That's better," the Tsarevich said, pleased. "You look much better when you smile. So . . . are you happy now you live here?"

I sighed. "No," I said.

He stared at me round-eyed. "Why not? Tsarskoe is the prettiest place in the world, except maybe for Livadia. Isn't Ania kind to you?"

"Oh, yes," I said. "It's not that. It's . . . " How could I tell this bright-eyed boy my shameful secret, that I was stupid?

"What's the matter, my dear?" asked Petrov. Then, turning to Alexei he said, "You must learn not to pester people with questions they may not want to answer, Alexei Nikolaevich."

He dared to speak to the Tsarevich that way? But Alexei hung his head. "I *do* ask a lot of questions," he said. "Sometimes people don't like it." Then he brightened. Putting his hand into his pocket, he brought out a fistful of objects. "Look, I'll show you my best things."

In his hand lay a coiled piece of copper wire, a stone with a white ring around it, two nails, a screw, a shard of metal — and a pencil stub. Even this little boy could write!

Alexei looked worried. "Don't you like my things?"

"They're very fine," I mumbled. "Do . . . Do you write a lot with the pencil?"

"This pencil?" he asked, sounding puzzled. "No, I only keep it because my friend Derevenko gave it to me. I'll give it to you, if you like," he added, holding it out.

I burst into tears. "I . . . I can't use it," I blubbered. "I can't write!"

"You can't write?" Alexei's eyes widened.

I shook my head, wiping my nose on my sleeve. "I'm too stupid to learn."

"Here, use this," said Petrov, offering a large white handkerchief.

I wiped my eyes, then gave my nose a hearty blow.

"That's better," he said, adding, "No, you keep it," as I made to hand it back. "Now, do you mean to tell me that you are crying because you don't know how to write?" he demanded, raising his bushy eyebrows. "Many people can't, unfortunately. What makes you care about it so much?"

"I . . . I . . . " Then the words rushed out. "Nobody

where I come from knows how to read or write. So I never thought about it. But then Grigory brought me to St. Petersburg and lots of people there could do it. And I wanted to, and I tried and tried. But I'm too stupid!"

"Now wait," he said. "Perhaps you haven't succeeded. But that doesn't mean you are stupid."

"But Ania tried to teach me, and I couldn't learn. So I must be."

"Ania!" Petrov mumbled something under his breath. I couldn't hear all of it but the end of it sounded like " . . . silly woman!"

"*You* could teach her, Pyotr Vassilievich," said Alexei. "Say you will!"

"Why not?" said Petrov. "If Alexandra Feodorovna approves. I often have free time . . . "

Alexei's face became solemn. "He means that I'm sick a lot and can't study."

I barely heard what he'd just said. "You really think I could learn?" I asked the tutor.

"Of course. Anyone can."

A great load lifted from my soul. Petrov was a real teacher. Surely he must know!

"Let's ask Mama right away," said Alexei, turning toward the palace.

Petrov put a hand on his arm. "Wait, now. Your mama is often very tired, you know. We must find the right moment."

Alexei considered. "Yes, you're right. Sometimes she says no if you ask at the wrong time. Even to Tatiana." He turned to me and held out his hand, "But don't you worry, Dunia Ivanovna," he said loftily. "Pyotr Vassilievich will be able to teach you. I promise!"

Not knowing what else to do with his hand, I shook it.

"When I'm Tsar," he added, "everyone in all the Russias will learn to read and write."

The moment they were out of sight, I twirled around and around until I tumbled, dizzy, into a heap of leaves. I was going to learn to read and write. The Tsarevich himself had said so!

7

Lessons

November – December, 1911

Two weeks later, I found myself sitting across a table from Anastasia. She was shooting stormy glances at me, and my heart sank. What had my foolish wagging tongue got me into now? My only comfort was that Marie was there too.

"I think it's lovely to have someone else," she said, beaming. "Usually we never do."

"Mama says we don't need anyone but ourselves," growled Anastasia.

Marie shrugged. "Mama herself said Dunia could come. So there!"

"Will Olga Nikolaevna and Tatiana Nikolaevna be coming too?" I asked, worried.

"The Big Pair? Of course not!" Anastasia snorted.

"They're older, you see," Marie explained. "So they do everything together. Anastasia and I are the Little Pair. We share everything — our room, our belongings, our lessons . . . We dress alike, too," she finished, pointing to their white blouses and blue skirts.

"Don't you mind?" I asked. "Having everything the same, I mean?"

Marie looked surprised. "Oh, no. Why would we?"

"Some sisters hate sharing their things."

"How bizarre!" drawled Anastasia

"'Bizarre' means 'strange'," explained Marie. "It's Anastasia's favourite word right now. We all have to put up with it until she gets tired of it."

"I'm bizarre, you're bizarre, everything is bizarre," chanted Anastasia, rolling about in her seat and wagging her head from side to side.

"What's bizarre, Anastasia Nikolaevna?" asked Petrov, coming into the room.

"*She's* bizarre," said Anastasia, sitting bolt upright and pointing at me. "Why is she here?"

"Alexandra Feodorovna said she may come until she learns to read and write," Petrov replied.

Anastasia made owl eyes. "She can't read and write? What a stupid girl!"

"Don't be horrid, Anastasia," chided Marie. "Don't mind her," she added, turning to me. "She just can't help being rude sometimes."

"Yes, I can!" snapped Anastasia, getting red in the face.

"I am very glad to hear it," said Petrov, "for it grieves me to hear you call anyone stupid. It is most unkind." He sat down. "Now, young ladies, let me see your homework."

Smiling sweetly at Petrov, Marie pushed a blank

sheet of paper across the table. "It was too hard, dear Pyotr Vassilievich," she said. "I tried, though. I really did."

Petrov sighed. "I fear you give in to your laziness too easily, Marie Nikolaevna."

Marie's blue saucer-eyes were wells of sadness. "I'm sorry. I'll try harder next time," she promised.

Anastasia groaned loudly. "You always say that, but it's the same thing every time." She pushed her own smudged and crumpled page across to Petrov.

He smoothed it out, and read it over, picking it up to peer more closely at it from time to time. "Very interesting," he said. "The way you express yourself is . . . original." He rubbed the end of his nose. "But I'd asked you to compare information from two different books."

Anastasia tossed her head. "Bah! You're always asking us to read books, Pyotr Vassilievich, but really, what's the use of them? It's people that count."

"As soon as Alexandra Feodorovna thinks you are old enough," the tutor replied, "you can go the rest of your life without reading another book. But for now you must do it." Taking a red pencil out of his pocket, he marked a big red zero on Marie's paper, and a one on Anastasia's. "I'm giving you something for having at least thought about the topic," he told her.

She jumped up and left the room. A moment later she returned with a huge bouquet of roses and lilies. She must have got them from a vase, as they were dripping. "Dear Pyotr Vassilievich," she said formally, "please accept these flowers."

Poor Petrov looked flustered. "Thank you, Anastasia Nikolaevna," he replied.

"*Now*," said Anastasia, her eyes dancing, "won't you give me a better mark?"

Marie giggled.

Petrov harrumphed and put down the bouquet. "I appreciate the flowers as a token of your esteem," he said. "But a one is what you deserve, and a one is what you get."

Anastasia flounced into her seat. She stuck out her lower lip and blew a puff of air, making her bangs flutter.

"As for you, Marie Nikolaevna," Petrov went on, "No work at all equals zero. I don't know what your father will say when he sees such marks."

"Papa knows she's a dunce," said Anastasia. "All Mashka wants to do is marry a soldier and have about twenty babies."

Marie blushed. "Shush, Anastasia. It's not proper to talk about having babies!"

So these grand duchesses weren't so smart after all. Well, long on hair, short on brains, I told myself, eyeing their flowing tresses and wishing my own hair would grow out faster.

Petrov sighed. "I shall set you each a new theme," he said. "I want at least one full page written before you go to lunch. Understood?"

Marie and Anastasia looked glum. Petrov wrote out their assignments, and they bent over the pages, chewing the ends of their pencils.

"Now, Dunia," said Petrov, turning to me. "Did

you learn the alphabet?" When I nodded, he said, "Show me," and pushed paper and a pencil across the table.

"Not bad!" he said when I had finished. "Why do you think you can't learn to read and write?"

"It's the words," I said. "There are too many."

"Too many? But you already know all the words." He peered at me under his shaggy brows. "You do speak Russian, don't you? Or do my ears deceive me?"

"Of course I do!" I said.

"The words you write are the words you speak, child! If you can't remember how the word looks, you sound it out. Each letter stands for a sound. Didn't Ania tell you that?"

"N-no . . . She just said the letters make the words."

Petrov rolled his eyes. "C-a-t. Cat," he said sounding the letters, then pronouncing the word very slowly. "Do you hear it? You run the sound of the letters together to make the words."

A great light dawned upon me. "I don't have to remember all the words?"

"No! Now, here are the sounds of the letters: ah, bay . . . " He moved his finger down my alphabet. Then he said, "How do you say the sounds in your name?"

"Duh . . . oo . . . nee . . . ah."

He circled the letters. "Now write the letter for each sound to make your name," he said. He showed me the letters again with the pencil, and I copied them down.

Suddenly there was my own name, in writing. "DUNIA!" I shouted.

"What are you making such a fuss about?" Anastasia was peering at me, her own lesson forgotten. "Any baby knows about sounds and letters."

"But I *didn't* know," I said. "Ania didn't tell me."

She shrugged. "Trust the Cow to get it wrong."

"Anastasia Nikolaevna!" said Petrov. "I'm ashamed of you."

"Oh, everyone calls her the Cow. You know they do."

"Such a sweet Cow," agreed Marie.

Petrov tried to look severe, but the ghost of a smile twitched the corner of his mouth.

I grinned. There *was* something cow-like about Ania's big, soft eyes.

As we left the room, Anastasia said under her breath. "You've wormed your way in here. But don't think that we like you."

I glowered at her. "Marie Nikolaevna likes me," I said.

"Mashka is a fat little bow-wow," snapped Anastasia. "She likes everybody."

"The Tsarevich likes me too," I shot back. "And the Tsarina said I could come."

Anastasia scowled. "Oh, Alexei! His head is full of silly notions. As for Mama, she'll do anything Alexei wants just now because his arm has been bleeding." Then she clapped her hand over her mouth. "Don't you tell anyone I said that," she demanded, backing away.

I stared at her. What did it matter if Alexei had hurt his arm? Boys always hurt themselves.

"If you tell, I'll make you pay, Dunia Ivanovna!" Anastasia scurried away down the corridor, and after that she didn't call me stupid anymore. What was she so afraid of?

My lessons went quickly now and soon I was reading simple stories. I wished Alexei knew. Then, one winter evening, I got a chance to tell him.

The telephone rang just as Ania was getting ready to go to the palace. "The Tsarina wants me to bring you with me," she said, hanging up. "I wonder why?"

In the woods outside the cottage, the ground was hard as iron, and the trees stood drifted deep in snow. But the Tsarina's room was warm, and the spicy smell of wood burning in the stove mixed with the smell of flowers. The Tsarina was sitting on her sofa turning the pages of a large album bound in green leather. At the other end of the room, Anastasia, Marie and Alexei sat on the floor, sticking pictures into more albums. Olga and Tatiana were at a small table doing the same thing.

"Here she is!" cried Alexei, jumping up and running over to us. "I made Mama invite you, Dunia. Pyotr Vassilievich says you can read and write now."

I grinned at him. "Yes, I can."

"Good, but don't get lazy. You have to keep working hard, you know."

"I will," I promised.

"We're working on our albums," he said. "Come

71

and see." Then, picking up a glossy black-and-white picture, "Here's a good one of Anastasia." He handed it to me. It showed her sticking her tongue out. "Just like her, don't you think?" he added.

Anastasia reached up and tweaked it out of my fingers. "Why show her *that* one?" she complained, peering at it. "You always take such stupid pictures anyway."

"Anastasia!" said Tatiana reproachfully.

"Well, he *does*." Anastasia gave her a saucy glance. "Don't be so governessy, Tatiana!"

Her sister shrugged. I hadn't seen the Big Pair since my first visit to the palace, and now I glanced shyly from one to the other. They looked much more grown up than Anastasia and Marie. Tatiana was very beautiful, and looked much like her mother. She had a way of lifting her chin when she spoke that made her look queenly. Olga wasn't as pretty, but she seemed more friendly.

"Look at these," Alexei said, handing me a stack of pictures.

"Where do you get them?" I asked, riffling through them.

"We *take* them. With that," he replied, pointing to a small black box that was sitting on a table. "It's a camera," he went on. "It . . . Well, I don't know how it works, but you put a special film in it. Outdoors in the sun you can take photographs of everything."

"You take a lot of them!" I said, for there were hundreds strewn across the floor.

Marie looked up, smiling. "We all have our own

cameras. Come and see our albums," she said, patting the floor beside her.

Alexei flopped down too, and began pawing through the heaps of photos. "It's hard to keep them in order," he said, his brow furrowed. "We take so many, and then there's the official photographer snapping away all the time too."

Alexei and Marie handed over their albums for me to look at, and after a moment Anastasia did too. Alexei's was neatly labelled, Marie's rather messy. Anastasia's was decorated with coloured drawings. I turned page after page. It was like magic. The pictures showed them doing ordinary things, not sitting posed and stiff. Here was Alexei beating a drum, Anastasia hanging upside down from a fence, Marie petting a kitten. The Big Pair walking along a dock, and the Tsarina wading on a rocky shore. And here was the back of a man swimming without any clothes on!

Marie looked over my shoulder, then quickly flipped the page. "Anastasia took that one of Papa. It was very bad of her. He didn't know she was there."

"Which album is best?" Anastasia demanded.

I hesitated. "They're all good — but I like the drawings in yours," I admitted grudgingly.

She looked pleased, but turned away quickly to hide it. "Why don't you read to us, Olga?" she asked, glancing up at her sister. "You must be nearly finished with your album."

Olga shook her head. "No, I've still a lot to do. But it would be nice to hear something."

"Don't ask me — I have an awful headache," said Tatiana, leaning back in her chair and pressing the palms of her hands against her eyes. "Let's hope Papa comes soon. He'll read to us."

I looked up from the albums. "I could *tell* you a story."

"You?" Anastasia stared at me.

"Yes," I said. "I know lots of them."

"Father Grigory tells us stories sometimes," said Olga.

"He told me one once," I said nodding. "Do you know the one about Maria Morevna?"

Olga shook her head. "Please tell us, Dunia."

"Yes," said Tatiana. Her grey eyes smiled down at me, and suddenly she didn't look so proud after all.

Alexei and Marie were nodding their heads. I glanced at Anastasia, who shrugged.

I settled myself cross-legged, hands in my lap. "Once long ago there was a tsarevich," I began.

"That's me!" exclaimed Alexei.

" . . . who had three sisters . . . "

"No, that's wrong," he said, frowning. "I have four sisters."

"Be quiet, Alexei, or we'll never get on," said Anastasia.

" . . . tsarevich who had *four* sisters," I said. "One day a raven asked to marry the eldest one — "

"That's you, Olga," said Anastasia. "Would you marry a raven if one asked you?"

"Now *you're* the one who's interrupting!" accused Marie.

"And the tsarevich said — " I did a voice for the tsarevich, then croaked the part of the raven.

"She's good, isn't she?" Alexei whispered to Marie.

"Shush!"

"So the tsarevich went to his eldest sister. She was very surprised to hear a raven wanted to marry her, but the bird flew in through the window and spoke to her so prettily that she fell in love with him at once. Soon the wedding was held, in great glory, and the raven departed with his bride. Then, the very next time the tsarevich went a-hunting, a hawk spoke to him . . . "

The story cast its spell, until at last I came to the end. "Everyone rejoiced, and the happy couples lived and prospered, to the glory of all the people," I finished, folding my hands in my lap.

"I liked the way it all came right in the end," sighed Marie, "with a husband for every sister."

"Bah!" scoffed Anastasia. "I liked the fight with the wizard best."

Alexei was thoughtful. "The tsarevich was brave, though he made a lot of mistakes."

"A tale well told," said a quiet voice behind us. "Grigory himself couldn't do better."

Olga's face lit up. "Papa!" she said, jumping up.

A man with a short brown beard and a moustache was standing just behind me. I'd seen his face in the photographs. It was the Batushka Tsar! I knelt and pressed my forehead to the floor.

"Get up, child. I don't like people to kneel," he said.

"I *told* her people don't carry on like that here," said Anastasia.

75

But I scarcely heard her, for I was looking into the eyes of the Tsar of All the Russias, and they were the saddest that I had ever seen. Blue and clear, with a shining light in them, but sad, so sad.

"I came in partway through your tale," he said. "My children looked so entranced that I wanted to hear for myself. Do you know many stories?"

"Yes, many," I said, nodding. "My mother told them to me."

"Then you must surely tell us more of them." He turned to the Tsarevich. "So, Alexei, it seems your protégé has even more talent than you thought."

Alexei reached up and patted me on the head. They all laughed. "Yes, she's very good, isn't she?" he said proudly. "And now she reads and writes too."

"Petrov told me," said the Tsar. "So . . . "

I caught my breath. Now he'd surely say that I didn't need to study with Petrov anymore!

" . . . she had better go on and learn as much as she can," he went on. "I don't think the Little Pair exactly stretch Petrov's talents. Perhaps an eager student will be an example to you, daughters," he said, smiling at Marie and Anastasia. Marie hung her head, and Anastasia shot me a killing glance from under her long eyelashes.

The Tsar went over to his wife's sofa. "How are you feeling, my dear?" he asked, leaning over and kissing her cheek.

She gazed up at him, her mouth blossoming into a smile, and the fretful lines vanishing from her face. "I'm a little tired, Nicky," she told him, squeezing his hand. "But not too bad."

"And our Ania," the Tsar added, turning and beaming down at her. "How is she tonight?"

"Well, Nikolai Alexandrovich. Well, quite well, actually . . . N-not too well," she stammered.

"What a lot of 'wells'! Which one is it?" he teased.

"Ania is perfectly fine," the Tsarina cut in.

"Ania Alexandrovna is in love with Papa," Marie whispered. "And Mama doesn't like it!"

Ania in love with the Tsar? She was certainly looking at him in a cow-like way. I watched as the children clustered around him, showing their albums. He had a kind word or a joke for each of them. So that is what a real father is like, I thought. Not a man with a stick.

The Tsarina looked on, smiling. The faces of the Tsar and the children kept turning to her like sunflowers to the sun. I could see that she was the heart, the centre of their world. As my own dear matushka had been . . . I swallowed a big lump in my throat.

"Tea!" exclaimed the Tsar, looking around and rubbing his hands. "I'm parched from working on so many papers. Where is our evening tea?"

Soon a huge silver samovar was wheeled in and everyone had tea. Then — far too soon for me — Ania got up to leave.

"Ania, you must bring Dunia with you every night now," commanded Alexei. "So she can tell us more stories."

"Please!" begged Marie.

"Yes, Ania," said Olga. "It's such a pleasant change for us."

Tatiana nodded. "Mama wouldn't mind, would you Mama?" Seating herself on the Tsarina's sofa, she patted her mother's hand.

The Tsarina, who had been looking doubtful, smiled and said, "If it would give you all pleasure, of course I don't mind."

Anastasia slouched in her chair with her arms crossed and her legs stuck out in front of her.

The Tsar's eyes twinkled. "And what about you, *malenkaya*? Don't you care for stories?"

"Of course she does," said Marie. "She's just being stubborn."

"Well . . . " Anastasia considered. "I suppose we can listen until we've heard all the stories she knows. *Then* we can send her away."

I grinned. Little did she know. When I ran out of stories, I'd just make up more!

8

Snapshots

January, 1912

"Why is the Tsar so sad?" I asked Jim one day. "You must know. You're right outside his door."

Jim looked both ways, but there was no one in sight except the other guard. "You're a regular demon for questions, aren't you?" he said.

"It doesn't cost anything to ask."

Jim sighed. "The Tsar's a good man. A real good man. But he's got a job that's just too big for him. The old tsar, his father — everyone says he was a tough customer. Big like a bear, and he could bend iron bars with his hands. That's what they say, anyway. He kept Russia nailed down tight."

"Our Batushka doesn't?"

Jim shook his head. "Can't. Oh, he wants to keep things the way his daddy did, but times have changed. Russia's got to change too. It's like a big pot, bubbling and boiling. It's going to boil right over some time. The Tsar does his best, according to his lights, but he sees trouble coming and he's right. That's why he looks so sad." He glanced at the other guard, who was scowling. "Now, I've said more than enough. You scat, little Dunia!"

I puzzled over what Jim had said. I was sorry our Batushka's job was too big for him, and I wondered what would happen when the pot boiled over. Not long afterward, I found Ania crying over the newspaper. "What is it?" I asked her.

"It's Father Grigory." She sighed. "The papers write such wicked things about him."

"What things?" I asked, peering over her shoulder. I could make out Grigory's name in a headline. There was another word beside it, and I spelled it out to myself: e-v-i-l. Evil. They thought Grigory was a bad man. Was he going to get into trouble? "What things?" I repeated.

"Things not proper for *you* to know," snapped Ania, whisking the paper away. "And . . . And they accuse him of giving bad advice to the Tsarina."

The Tsarina *did* seem to believe whatever Grigory told her. "Does she give Grigory a lot of money?" I asked.

Ania looked shocked. "Certainly not! She doesn't give him any at all. Why would she?"

"Other people do," I pointed out. "Marochka said so."

Ania flushed. "People go to Grigory with their troubles," she said. "He spends hours trying to help them, so why shouldn't they pay him a little something? He gives the money away to the poor."

Maybe, but he keeps plenty for himself, I thought, remembering all his rubles.

After that, Ania tried to hide the newspaper from me. I managed to sneak a look sometimes, and often saw Grigory's name on the front page. But I couldn't read well enough yet to make much sense of the stories. I kept trying, though, because I was worried. If Grigory *did* get into trouble, what would happen to me?

My lessons with Petrov continued. Tatania sometimes joined us now, and when she did, Anastasia had to behave. The rest of the time, hardly a lesson passed without some kind of prank. One day she arrived dressed up like a chimney sweep with her face blackened, and sat that way until Tatiana, arriving late, threw up her hands in horror and dragged her out. Another day, she found a way to balance a paper bag full of flour over the door, so that when poor Petrov entered, it tumbled down on him, powdering his head and shoulders white. Another time, she put an air cushion on his chair. When the poor man sat down a loud rude noise was heard. The little shvipsik always kept a straight face through all her mischief, but her wicked blue eyes would dance. Other times, she would suddenly burst out laughing, as if she had thought of the funniest thing in the world. Well, people who tickle themselves can laugh when they like.

"Anastasia, you must stop teasing Petrov," Marie told her one day when the tutor went out of the room. "You're making his life miserable."

Anastasia made a face at her.

"If you don't stop," threatened Marie, getting up, "I'll do this!" Seizing Anastasia by the waist, she hoisted her into the air.

My mouth dropped open. Marie must be incredibly strong!

"Put me down, Mashka!" cried Anastasia, struggling.

"Not until you promise to behave," said Marie, lifting her higher still. "Take your time. I can keep this up as long as you like!"

"All right, all right, I promise!" But back on her feet, Anastasia turned sulky. "It's not fair," she said. "Just because I'm small and you're so strong."

"Too bad for you," said Marie grinning. "And remember — you promised!"

After that, Petrov's life got easier for awhile.

I saw the family more and more outside my lesson times too. Often now when Ania's telephone rang, the call would be for me.

"Dunia?" Alexei's voice crackled through the wire one bright afternoon. "We're going to build a snow mountain by the little lake. Come and help us!"

"I can't imagine why they need *you* for their games," Ania pouted.

Bundling myself up in my warmest clothes, I scampered through the snowy woods. Igor, who was clearing paths, waved his shovel as I trotted by. "Going to play with Batushka's children?" he asked. "Good, good. They need more playmates."

When I reached the lake, the Tsar and the Big Pair

had gone off for a walk. "Come and see Vanka," Alexei cried, dragging me over to a grizzled donkey harnessed to a sledge. "He's mine, you know. Papa bought him from a circus."

The lop-eared beast thrust his muzzle into my pocket.

"He's looking for treats. *I* know what he likes," said Anastasia, taking out a rubber ball. Vanka seized it and chewed it, closing his eyes.

"I had a horse once," I said. "Well, he wasn't really mine, but I liked him. I called him Turnip."

"Turnip? What a funny name," said Alexei, jumping up and down to keep warm. "What happened to him, then?"

"Grigory sold him at Tiumen," I said.

At the mention of Grigory's name, all their faces became solemn. "We're not supposed to talk about Father Grigory," said Anastasia, frowning. "Mama told us not to."

"But Dunia *knows* him," Marie pointed out. "So it must be all right, mustn't it?"

"Forget Father Grigory," ordered Alexei, picking up a shovel. "Let's build our mountain!"

"I'm in charge," cried Anastasia, dashing on ahead. "It was my idea!"

She chose a spot by the lake, and we shovelled snow into a mound. Then we piled more snow on Vanka's sledge and had him drag it over. When the Big Pair and the Tsar got back, they helped us, and soon the pile of snow was higher than our heads.

"That's enough for today," said the Tsar. "By

tomorrow it will be frozen solid and we can build it higher."

"I'll ask Petrov to help us," said Anastasia. "And Zhilik and Gibbsy too. Maybe it'll make them forget about giving us homework!"

The next day, Petrov came. He brought Monsieur Gilliard, the French tutor, and Mr. Gibbes, the English tutor. Anastasia ran around giving everybody orders, and the pile of snow grew higher and higher. It really looked like a mountain now. The day after, it was ready to be iced. Now Vanka's sledge pulled buckets of water that we filled through a hole chopped in the ice of the lake. The Tsar, the tutors, and Olga clambered to the top of the hill to pour bucket after bucket down its steeper slope, turning it into a glistening sheet of ice.

After another day of pouring and waiting, came the sliding! The Tsar, Alexei and the Big Pair went down on toboggans, and the rest of us on wooden sleds. Anastasia teased Petrov until he forgot his dignity and sailed down on a sled far too small for him, his whiskers blowing back over his shoulders. Then she dragged a huge silver tea-tray to the top and shot down the slope backwards. The wind blew her skirts up, showing her knickers, and everyone howled with laughter.

"There's one for my album!" said Olga, lowering her camera. She glanced down at me, her blue-grey eyes beaming, and little tendrils of fair hair escaping from under her fur hat. Then she held out the camera. "Why don't you take one with all of us in it, little Dunia?" she asked.

I seized the camera, for I'd been dying to take pictures.

"Stand with your back to the sun," Olga told me. "You press the shutter here." Then she ran to join the rest, crying, "Come, everyone. For once we can all be in the picture!"

I peered into the camera. There they all were, arms linked, with the snow mountain behind them. I pressed the button and the camera clicked.

Olga came back, smiling. "Your very first snapshot," she said. "Would you like to have it?"

"Yes, please, Olga Nikolaevna!"

"I'll be developing the film tomorrow," she said. "You could come and watch."

She knew the magic of photographs! "Could I?"

"Why not? Come and find me after your lessons. I'll be in Mama's room."

We slid down the mountain again and again, until the light began to fade. "Tomorrow! Say we can come again tomorrow, Papa," Alexei begged, as we trudged back to the palace in the silvery-blue dusk.

"If this fine cold weather lasts," replied the Tsar. "And if your mother agrees."

Why wouldn't she? I wondered. "Doesn't the Tsarina like you to slide?" I said to Marie.

"She . . . She worries, you know. About Alexei." Marie's smile faded from her rosy face.

Anastasia, who was tramping along behind her, gave her a poke between the shoulders. "You're not supposed to talk about it, Mashka," she said.

What a lot of things they weren't supposed to talk

about. First Grigory, and now this.

The next day, as soon as my lesson was finished, I ran downstairs to Alexandra Feodorovna's sitting room. Pausing in the doorway, I bobbed a curtsey to a lady-in-waiting. "Please," I said. "Olga Nikolaevna said to come and ask for her."

The lady-in-waiting looked down her nose as if I smelled bad. But she went over to a carved screen set around the Tsarina's sofa and said, "Excuse me, Olga Nikolaevna, there's an odd-looking child here asking for you. Shall I send her away?"

"That's Dunia," said Olga's voice from behind the screen. "I promised to show her how to develop photographs."

I heard the Tsarina murmur something. Her voice sounded fretful.

"Oh, Mama! It won't take long," said Olga, coming around the screen and picking up her camera. The moment we were out of sight, she hoisted her long skirt and ran down the corridor. "We must hurry," she said. "Mama's not well today, and she wants me to stay with her."

She opened the door of a room along the hall and switched on a reddish light inside. "This is our darkroom," she explained, closing the door behind us. "You mustn't take the film out of the camera in ordinary light, or you'll spoil the pictures."

Magic was all around me. I could feel it! Olga poured liquid from jars into two dishes. I sniffed. It even smelled like magic, a tang that went right up my nose and behind my eyes.

She unwound the roll of film and laid it in the first dish. "This is where the magic happens," she said. She understood about magic, then! I gazed down at the strip of film. In each small square, tiny images were beginning to form.

Olga handed me a piece of curved glass with a handle. "If you look through the magnifying glass you can actually see the pictures emerging," she said.

"But . . . It's all backwards!" For the snow mountain was black with white figures in front of it.

"Later, when the picture is printed, it comes out right," Olga explained.

The images became clearer. "There's Anastasia Nikolaevna," I said. "Look, you can see her behind."

"Got her, got her!" Olga crowed. "She'll be so embarrassed! And look," she added, "there's the photo you took."

"Can I have it now?" I asked.

She shook her head. "Not yet." She lifted the wet film into the other dish and swished it back and forth. "There. Now we hang it up to dry," she said, fastening the strip to a little line strung in one corner. "Another time, I'll show you how to make a print you can keep."

I sighed with pleasure. This was the best magic in the world, and I was going to learn it!

9

Cakes and Secrets

April – May, 1912

Spring came early that year. By April the snow lay in melting patches on the lawns and terraces, and the breeze felt soft and damp. It was mud time — too warm for winter fun, but too chilly to do much of anything else.

"Soon we're going to Li-va-di-a," chanted Alexei, stamping through a puddle in the palace courtyard.

"Where's that?" I asked, jumping back to avoid a soaking.

"Never mind," jeered Anastasia, strolling along behind us with her hands in her pockets. "You aren't going."

Alexei stopped short and stared at her. "Dunia could come to Livadia," he said. "Why not?" He gave the puddle another stamp.

Anastasia scowled. "There you go again! You're always bringing her into everything," she grumbled.

"Why shouldn't I, if I want to?" he challenged.

"She's my pro — Well, whatever Papa said she was."

"Protégé," explained Marie. "It's French. Zhilik says it means someone you look after."

Alexei nodded solemnly. "That's right. She's mine, and I'm going to look after her."

"That's silly!" sneered Anastasia.

"You're just jealous. You don't have a protégé," Alexei retorted.

Anastasia turned beet red. "I am not jealous!" she said angrily. "I just hate it when you make such a fuss over her. Anyway, Mama will say no. She only wants *us* at Livadia."

"But Ania goes everywhere with Mama," Marie put in. "So why can't we have our friend too? It's only fair."

"She's not my friend," muttered Anastasia.

"She would be if you weren't rude to her all the time," Alexei shot back. "Anyway," he went on, "I want Dunia to come. I'm going to get Tatiana to ask Mama."

"And I'm going to tell Mama I don't want her to go!" snapped Anastasia. They were both bright red now, and their eyes were blazing.

What a spoilsport Anastasia was! I *would* go to Livadia, wherever it was, just to spite her.

"Anastasia Nikolaevna," I said in a sugary voice.

"What?"

"Remember when we talked — oh, a long time ago — about you know who?" I asked. "And you said I'd better not tell?" I held my breath. Would my threat actually work?

She glared at me, then she turned her back and stalked off.

Alexei shrugged. "Nastasia is jealous," he said. "I know she is. But I'm sure Mama will let you come with us."

I felt as if there were two me's. The good me felt mean for making Anastasia think I'd tell on her. But the bad me said that it served her right for being so nasty.

God was watching me, though, because the very next day, Ania broke her ankle. She couldn't go to Livadia, so neither could I. God just didn't want me to go, I told myself, but I wondered why He hadn't broken *my* ankle.

Poor Ania was miserable. Her ankle hurt horribly and she missed seeing the family. Feeling guilty, I tried to be good to her. Day after day I gave her back rubs, and sponged her with cologne. I brought her tea tray and fetched her chocolates, even though she didn't always offer me one. I read the newspaper headlines to her, though I still stumbled over many words, and when she got tired of that, I told her stories. She liked the same ones Marie did — those with love and happy endings.

Once, when I brought a cold cloth for her forehead, she squeezed my hand. "I'm . . . I'm glad you're here, Dunia," she said. "I am less lonely now. Father Grigory was right."

I squeezed her hand back. I was glad she didn't want to be rid of me anymore. That night I thanked God for making Ania like me, and I asked Him to make sure my matushka knew. She would be happy that someone cared for me in this strange place.

When Ania didn't need me, I roamed the park feeling lonely, my boots sinking into slush. It felt as if all the heart had gone out of Tsarskoe.

Jim said it was always like that when the family went away. I'd tracked him down in a distant wing of the palace, packing a giant trunk. He said he was going home for a long visit with his own family. I asked when he was coming back.

"Can't say for sure," he replied. "Just look at the newspapers. All these European countries building warships, making big guns. Trying them out, too — a little war here, a little war there. Trouble is coming. Big trouble." He shot me a glance. "It's coming here in Russia for sure, little Dunia. You watch out!"

With him gone I was lonelier than ever. More weeks dragged by. Then one morning Ania's telephone rang. "Da?" I bellowed into the mouthpiece, worried that my voice wouldn't squeeze through the wires.

"Dunia?" said Grigory's voice. "Where is Ania?"

"Upstairs. She has a broken ankle."

"She must come to the telephone."

I raced upstairs. "It's Grigory," I panted. "On the telephone. He wants to talk to you — even though I told him about your ankle!"

I thought she'd say no, but she didn't. Instead, she sat up and swung her good leg over the side of the bed. "Help me with the crutches, Dunia," she said, wincing.

She stopped at the top of the stairs. "What can I do?" she wailed.

"Go down on your rump," I said.

"Don't use rude words, Dunia!" she snapped. But she did it, moaning all the way. "Father Grigory?" she gasped when she reached the telephone. "What? But the Tsarina is still away!" She paused, then she said, "Dunia? To Petersburg?"

Go to Petersburg? "Let me! Let me! I can do it!" I clamoured, tugging at her sleeve.

"Hush, Dunia!" Another pause. "Yes, if it's that important, I'll find a way."

She decided that Igor would take me. He was delighted. "A day off," he said, winking.

The line outside Grigory's door was longer than ever. Igor waited downstairs while Nikolai ushered me up ahead of everyone else. People growled and gave me black looks.

Grigory was even more finely dressed than before, his great gold cross gleaming on his chest. "Well, my flea, you look better than when I saw you last," he said, looking me up and down.

"You look terrible," I said, staring up at him. For his eyes were watery and his face was pasty pale. His beard, long and unkempt, was speckled with bits of food.

He frowned. "Mind your tongue," he said. Then, putting on a pious expression, he added, "I have been up all night praying at a sick woman's bedside."

Liar, I thought. My father had often looked as Grigory did, and he got that way in the tavern, not praying at bedsides.

My thoughts must have showed on my face, for Grigory's eyes narrowed, and the wolf looked out. "Remember, my flea," he said, "it was I who placed you with Ania. You are there only to serve me. Behave yourself, or I'll send you back to Pokrovskoe in a basket!"

I was never going back to Pokrovskoe if I could help it! "Yes, Grigory Efimovich," I said.

He sat down in an armchair. "Now look at me, Dunia, and listen," he said, holding my eyes with his. "There are wicked men in our Orthodox Church who hate me and want to destroy me. They fear my influence over Matushka and Batushka. Well, I'm going to deal with them."

Wicked men in our Holy Mother Church? How could it be?

"I am going to give you a list of names. I want you to make a copy, and give it to Ania. She must give it to Matushka as soon as she returns from Livadia. There's not a moment to lose. Our Little Mother understands that God will not hear my prayers for the Tsarevich if she allows these evil ones to prosper in His Holy Church."

Grigory and his prayers! Why did they matter so much? "Why don't I just give your list to Ania?" I asked. "Or you could tell her on the telephone."

He shook his head. "There must be nothing in my writing," he said. "And evil ones may listen in on the telephone line." He handed me a scrap of paper. I read it over, struggling to make out the crudely-scrawled names. Grigory wrote far worse than I did!

The first name was Bishop Hermogen, and there were four others.

"Write them down," he ordered, pointing to paper and pencil laid ready on the table.

I obeyed.

"Good," he said. Taking his own list back, he tore it into tiny bits. Then he yawned and scratched himself under the arms. The wolf was gone, and he was just plain Grigory again.

"So what did the old devil want?" Igor wanted to know when I came downstairs.

I shrugged. "I didn't understand," I lied.

As soon as we reached Ania's cottage I gave the list to her, but I didn't forget about it. A bishop was a very holy man. I didn't believe Bishop Hermogen could be evil, no matter what Grigory said. More likely Grigory was the evil one. The newspapers said so!

Now each day was warmer than the last, and thousands of lilac bushes in the park burst into bloom, drenching the air with their sweetness. With the warm weather, the family came back from Livadia. Because Ania couldn't go to the palace, the Tsarina and OTMA came to have tea in her little house. I helped Vera take their hats and wraps. Anastasia ignored me, but Tatiana gave me a friendly nod, and Marie squeezed my arm. Olga said, "We've taken hundreds of snapshots, Dunia. You must come and help develop them."

"Yes, please!" I said. Then, "Couldn't Alexei Nikolaevich come today?"

"He hasn't been well," said Olga. "Didn't Ania tell you?"

"But he's all better now," Anastasia broke in. "Father Grigory prayed for him."

Grigory again!

Anastasia was gloating over the cakes on the tea table. "I do love having tea at your house," she cried, throwing herself on Ania and giving her a bear hug. "Why don't you break your ankle more often? Break both of them! Then we could come to tea all the time."

Ania patted her hair back into place. "Now, don't tease, Anastasia Nikolaevna," she whimpered. "It's not kind. If you only knew how I've suffered!"

"Oh, poor, poor, poor Ania," said Anastasia. "But we love, love, love you for your cakes!" She pressed her fingertip to her chin, pondering. "Well, if not another ankle, why not a leg?" she suggested with a wicked grin.

"Anastasia!" said Tatiana. "If you go on like that you'll get no cakes at all!"

"Oh, you're such a governess, a grim, ghastly governess," chanted Anastasia, stamping her feet to the rhythm of her words.

"You see, we get such boring teas at home," sighed Marie. "Nothing but hot bread and butter. No fancy sandwiches, no cakes . . ."

"Good thing for you, fat Bow-wow, or you'd be even fatter," muttered Anastasia, with a quick glance to make sure Tatiana hadn't overheard.

"Why can't you have anything you like?" I asked.

Alexandra Feodorovna looked up smiling. "You'd think the Tsarina of All the Russias could have cakes with her tea if she wanted to, now wouldn't you, Dunia? But it's not so easy." She sighed. "For hundreds of years, the palace has served hot bread and butter, and the custom can't be changed, or so they tell me!"

"Well let's make the most of it now," urged Anastasia, flipping open her napkin. And soon every plate was empty.

Ania sat beaming at them all, but her face fell when the Tsarina told her that they had to go away again.

"We're going on the *Standart*," Marie said. "Uncle Willy is coming to visit, and Papa has to meet him,"

"Nasty Uncle Willy," said Anastasia, grimacing.

"You shouldn't speak of Uncle Willy that way," said Olga. But she said it as if she thought she should, rather than as if she really meant it.

"Well, he is nasty. You know he is," insisted Anastasia. Jumping up, the shvipsik took a turn around the room, strutting along with her cheeks puffed out, making trumpet noises through her fist. "My dearest Nicky," she proclaimed, thumping her chest. "Let me tell you what to do, as one emperor to another, boom, boom!"

They all burst out laughing. The little imp *was* funny.

"Uncle Willy is the Emperor of Germany," Olga explained to me. "He's always trying to bully Papa and tell him what to do. It's awfully rude!"

"I've missed you all so much!" sighed Ania. "When are you leaving?"

"Very soon," said the Tsarina. "But never mind, Ania," she added, patting her hand. "Now you're up on crutches there's no reason why you shouldn't come too. You can come aboard in the bosun's chair."

Ania brightened. "Aboard the *Standart*? Oh, how lovely!" Then, to my delight, she added, "And Dunia? May I bring her? I wouldn't know how to do without her now."

I held my breath. Would the Tsarina say no?

But she smiled serenely. "Didn't our dear Father Grigory say it would be so?" she asked. "He said she would be good for us all, and he was right. Of course Dunia may come." Turning to me, she added, "Marie has missed you at her lessons. And Alexei has been asking after his protégé."

"Oh, please say hello to him for me," I said.

"What's the *Standart?*" I asked Ania when they had gone.

"It's a yacht, child. The most beautiful yacht in the world. We'll go up north to meet it at Peterhof."

Ania sent to St. Petersburg the very next morning for new clothes for me to wear on the *Standart* — sailor blouses and skirts, and striped jerseys. Never had I had so many things before. I tried them all on, craning my neck to see all sides of myself in the mirror. My hair had grown out in a curly mop, and I really didn't look too bad. If only I could grow taller than Anastasia! Folk say that hopping on one leg makes you grow, so for weeks and weeks I'd been hopping round and round Ania's dining room table. But it hadn't worked yet.

I was so excited about going on the *Standart* that I didn't think about Grigory. Then, the day before we left, I was reading the paper to Ania, and I saw a familiar name. "Bishop Hermogen exiled to Siberia," I read aloud. Then I stopped and gazed at Ania wide-eyed.

She nodded. "Yes," she said. "It seems terrible that a bishop could be wicked, but Grigory truly sees into the hearts of men."

So already the first of Grigory's "enemies" had been struck down!

10

Islands

June, 1912

Peterhof was a park with many palaces, even bigger than Tsarskoe Selo. No sooner had Ania and I arrived than Alexei sent for me. He was in a tower room with big glass windows looking out over the sea. Anastasia sat hunched over a checkerboard on a low table beside him. She made a face when she saw me.

Alexei looked thin and pale, but his eyes were as merry as ever. "Hello, protégé," he said, grinning. "I'm going to test you to see if you've been working hard while I've been away."

Anastasia groaned loudly. "Oh, who cares?" she said.

"I do. Run away, Nastasia," Alexei ordered, flapping his hand at her. "We'll finish our game later. I have business with Dunia."

"Bah," she said. But she got up and strolled out onto the balcony, where she picked up a long tube-like thing and stood squinting through it.

Alexei had me read a story aloud out of his book.

I did my best, though I made some mistakes.

"Not bad," he said, when I had finished. "What about your writing, though?" He thought for a moment, then he brightened. "I know!" he said. "You can write a story for me. A special one, mind, not one you tell the others."

"I'll try," I said doubtfully. For the whole idea of writing down stories was still strange to me.

"Take all the time you like," he said graciously.

Just then, Anastasia gave a loud cheer. "Hurrah! The *Standart*'s coming!" she shouted. "I can see her!"

"Oh, where?" I cried, jumping up. For my head was so full of going on the *Standart* that I could hardly think of anything else.

Alexei and I dashed out onto the balcony. "Let Dunia try Papa's telescope, Nastasia," he said. "Close one eye when you look," he added.

Anastasia frowned, but she handed over the telescope. I closed one eye and peered through it. For a moment I saw nothing, and then there was the ship, right up close. It was all shiny black with a pointed bow and a gold stripe along its side. As the ship turned I could see a great gold double eagle glittering on the stern.

"Oh, it's beautiful," I breathed. "When are we going on it?"

"You must call ships 'she', not 'it'," Alexei insisted. "That's proper, you know. And we'll be going aboard tomorrow, to meet Uncle Willy at sea."

"I can't wait," I sighed, giving up the telescope to him.

"You'll be sorry. You're going to be seasick," jeered Anastasia with a wicked grin. "The ship tosses UP and down, UP and down," she went on, making swooping movements with her finger. "The waves, you know. And your stomach goes whooops!"

We went aboard the *Standart* the very next morning. Ania turned white when they tied her into a bosun's chair — a kind of sling — and swung her aboard. The rest of us scrambled up ladders on the side. The sea was choppy and the deck swooped up and down under my feet, just as Anastasia had said it would. My stomach did begin to feel like whooops. But I caught her watching me out of the corner of her eye, so I pretended I was fine.

Then Emperor Willy's big iron ships appeared out of the mist, and the *Standart's* cannon boomed in welcome. "I'm killed!" shrieked Anastasia, rolling her eyes wildly. Clutching her chest with both hands, she staggered a few steps and toppled to the deck, where she lay flat on her back with her tongue lolled out. The white-clad officers of the gun crew stared down at her from the upper deck, horrified.

"Get up, you ridiculous child!" The Tsarina rapped the deck sharply with the tip of her lacy parasol, and Alexei went over and prodded Anastasia in the ribs with the toe of his shoe.

The shvipsik sat up, grinning. "Pretty good, wasn't I?" she asked.

I had a good look at the Emperor Willy when he came aboard the *Standart*. He wasn't nearly as impressive as our tsar, I thought, as he strutted by.

Anastasia's imitation of him had been just right. She *was* clever. Too bad she was so mean.

After two days of meetings and banquets, Uncle Willy took himself and his great big ships back to Germany. The *Standart* got underway at once, and the shore sank out of sight behind us. When I woke up the next morning, the ship wasn't moving, and I put my head out the porthole.

Over the salt smell of the sea, another scent, spicy and tangy, tickled my nose. The smell of the forest. We were anchored in a deep bay, with wooded shores stretching away into the distance. Right ahead of us, an island of red rock with a cap of pine trees seemed to float on the deep green water. The sun was just coming up, and its rays touched the trunks of the trees, painting them with gold.

I tried to wake Ania up, but she just moaned. Her stomach had been going whooops quite a lot. So I dressed and hung out the porthole again. Soon there was a tap at the door. Alexei was outside, with Marie behind him.

"Come on, Dunia," said Alexei. "We're going ashore."

"Ania always stays aboard with Mama," explained Marie.

The others were waiting for us on deck. "But where are we?" I asked Alexei as we scrambled down the ladder to a small boat.

"Finland!" he said, grinning.

"This is the bay of the *Standart*," announced Anastasia. "It's our own very special place."

The boat put us ashore in a little cove. At once the others took their stockings and shoes off and wiggled their toes in the yellow sand. I did too. It felt warm and grainy between my toes.

"Let's hunt for mushrooms," the Tsar announced, pulling baskets out of the boat. "If you want breakfast, you're going to have to work for it!"

Mushrooms! I grabbed a basket and scampered up the beach to the woods. I stopped on the edge, taking a deep breath of the forest smell, then I looked around. I knew just the sort of places mushrooms like, places with pockets of deep soil, where the sun didn't reach. Soon I was popping juicy morsels into my basket.

"You needn't take all the good ones," Anastasia complained. Her basket was almost empty.

"Look, there are lots over there," I said, pointing to a patch of shaggy ones.

"Oh, *those* are no good," she said, tossing her head. Then, bending over, "Why here's a real beauty that you missed!" And she reached for a pale one poking through the grass.

"Not that one!" I cried, grabbing her arm. "It's poison!"

She glared at me. "What do you know, anyway?" she said, bending to pick it.

"Don't touch it, Anastasia!" It was the Tsar, right behind us. "Dunia is right. That one is deadly. But the ones over there are excellent." He pointed to the ones I had showed her before.

Casting a black glance at me, Anastasia went over to pick them.

When we got back to the beach someone had got a fire of twigs and driftwood going. Out of the boat came a frying pan, butter, onions, eggs and bread. It was the best breakfast I'd ever eaten. But when I put my plate down for a moment, Anastasia kicked sand over it.

And that was just the beginning. Later, when we were getting ready to go exploring, I discovered that my shoes and socks had disappeared. I found them under a rock, stuffed with smelly seaweed and dead crabs. And so it went all morning. A shower of bark on my hair, pine needles down my neck, and a big splotch of sticky pine pitch on the back of my new jersey. The others didn't seem to notice. Anastasia was grinning from ear to ear.

At last I had had enough. Running on ahead of the others, I stooped and filled my pockets with dirt and pine needles from the forest floor. Then I climbed the nearest tree.

The others passed right beneath me.

"Where's Dunia?" I heard Alexei ask.

"Up ahead somewhere. We'll catch up with her," said Olga.

I stayed where I was and waited for Anastasia to come looking for me. I knew she would. Sure enough, five minutes later she came back down the path, looking sharply to left and right.

"Up here," I called down to her.

Her mouth dropped open. "How'd you get way up there?" she demanded.

"I climbed," I replied.

She frowned. "Well, I didn't think you flew. But how did you do it?"

"It's easy. Come over here and I'll show you!"

She came to the base of the tree, and stared up. Digging into my pockets, I let her have both handfuls of dirty pine needles right in the face. They stuck in her hair and went into her eyes and mouth.

"Come down, you coward!" she spluttered.

"I'm no coward!" I climbed down a couple of branches, then slid the rest of the way. The moment my feet touched the ground, she went for me, pulling my hair and shoving me hard against the tree. I gave back as good as I got. Losing our footing on the slippery pine needles, we fell to the ground, still locked together, and rolled over and over, scratching and clawing like a couple of cats.

"You spoil everything!" Anastasia hissed.

"You're mean!" I spat.

"Stop it, both of you!" Hands seized us, jerking us apart. When I got the dirt out of my eyes, I discovered that Olga had grabbed me by both arms. Tatiana had hold of Anastasia by the waist. She was still trying to get at me, her arms flailing like windmills. Alexei and Marie were standing behind Tatiana, round-eyed.

"Stop it, Nastasia!" ordered Tatiana, giving her a shake.

The two of us glared at each other. I was still furious, but a terrible cold feeling was growing in the pit of my stomach. Now they'd send me away for sure, Grigory or no Grigory. Maybe they'd even shoot me!

"What happened?" asked Olga, letting me go.

I stared down at my feet. What good would it do to tell? It would make no difference now.

"I don't like her," muttered Anastasia. "She pushes her way in everywhere. This is *our* island, our special place!"

"But she's our friend," said Marie. "Isn't she, Alexei?"

He nodded. "And she's my protégé too. See here, Nastasia," he said. "This won't do. I saw you being mean to her all morning. I meant to stop you, but I couldn't catch up with you. It serves you right if she got angry."

She scowled at him, but said nothing.

Tatiana raised her eyebrows. "So that's it!" She turned to Olga. "I think this is something for the Big Pair to decide, don't you?" she asked. "*I* think we should say nothing about it to Papa or Mama or anyone else."

Olga nodded. "I agree. Nastasia, let this be a lesson to you. You always torment people because you know you can get away with it. That's cowardly!"

Anastasia's face turned bright red. She opened her mouth to say something, then hung her head and kicked at the ground.

"But Dunia," Tatiana added, her face grave, "You really mustn't pummel grand duchesses. No matter how much they deserve it!"

"I . . . I won't, Tatiana Nikolaevna," I stammered.

"We'd better clean them up before Papa sees them," said Marie, pulling a comb out of her pocket.

Alexei ran to dip everybody's handkerchiefs in a stream and they scrubbed our hands and faces, while Marie combed the bark out of our hair.

"Not too bad," said Tatiana, cocking her head and looking us over. "Dunia has a scratch on one cheek. Papa won't notice, but we'd better hope Mama doesn't! Now march, both of you."

The Big Pair led the way, and Marie and Alexei fell in behind us. As we went along, Olga whispered something to Tatiana, and they laughed. They thought it was funny!

Fortunately, the Tsar didn't seem to notice anything amiss. I'd hoped to slip straight down to our cabin to change, but the Tsarina and Ania were sitting on the deck under a canvas when we clambered over the side of the *Standart*.

"Dunia! What on earth have you done to your clothes?" demanded Ania, eyeing my torn and stained jersey.

The Tsarina put down her book and peered at me. "Why, the child has a scratch on her cheek," she said. "What happened, Dunia?"

Behind her back, the Big Pair exchanged glances.

"Oh, we were playing a game," said Anastasia. "And Dunia tripped over a root and fell, didn't you, Dunia?"

"Yes," I nodded, and she flashed me an approving glance.

"I see," said Alexandra Feodorovna, raising an eyebrow. She didn't ask any more about it, but I had the uncomfortable feeling that we hadn't fooled her at all.

11

Spala

September – October, 1912

The carriage jolted along the sandy road through the forest, and I breathed in the woodsy smell of the huge trees that loomed close around us. We were on our way to Spala, the Tsar's hunting lodge in Poland. I sighed. Though I had lived with Ania for nearly a year now, I could never get used to how the Tsar's family moved around so much. They were like birds with a different nest for every season.

A glade opened ahead of us. Why, Spala wasn't a palace at all — it was a great gloomy wooden house. At the sight of it, goosebumps stood up on my arms, and I crossed myself.

"What's the matter?" asked Ania.

"The house. It's so, so . . . dark," I faltered. For I couldn't put into words what I felt.

"Of course it's dark. It's in the middle of the forest. And it's old and cramped." Ania sighed. "I'm not fond of Spala myself. But the Tsar comes here to hunt with the Polish nobles."

As Ania had said, Spala was cramped, with tiny rooms and narrow passages. Dozens of servants were falling over each other while they tried to carry out their duties.

"Here you are!" cried Marie, leaning over the railing of the first floor landing. "Hurry up, Dunia. Alexei has been asking for you."

The Tsarevich was lying on a sofa, with Anastasia perched on a windowsill behind him.

"Hullo, Dunia," he said, grinning. Anastasia nodded to me. Since Finland, we weren't exactly friends, but we weren't enemies anymore.

"Are you sick, Alexei Nikolaevich?" I asked.

"No," said Anastasia. "He just did something stupid."

"It wasn't stupid," protested Alexei. "I was jumping into a rowboat, and I bruised myself."

"You shouldn't have been jumping at all," Anastasia shot back.

Just then a deep horn sounded in the woods. "It's the hunters!" she cried. "I'm going to find out how many stags they got." She ran out, banging the door behind her.

The next morning, the Big Pair went walking, and the Tsarina and Ania took Alexei off for a carriage ride. The Little Pair and I took baskets and walked into the forest looking for mushrooms. In a glade near the edge of the woods, we came upon a perfect ring of them.

"Don't pick them!" I took a step backward, crossing myself. I put my hand in my pocket and touched an iron nail I always kept with me.

"*Now* what's the matter?" groaned Anastasia. "These aren't poisonous — I know they're not!"

"Wood spirits," I whispered. "This is their ring. If you touch it, they'll put bad luck on you." I held out the nail. "Spirits are afraid of iron. If you touch this the bad luck won't harm you."

Marie touched the nail right away.

"I don't believe such bosh," said Anastasia, but she touched it anyway. Then she shrugged. "Well, if you won't let us pick the mushrooms," she went on, "you can teach me to climb trees. You said you would — *you* know when." And she gave me a rascally grin.

The three of us came out of the woods an hour later, brushing bark from our hair. A crowd had gathered at the front door of Spala, and someone was being lifted out of a carriage, then carried up the stairs.

"Alexei!" cried Anastasia, turning pale. Dropping her basket, she took to her heels, with Marie right behind her. I caught up with them outside Alexei's room. Ania was there, wringing her hands, tears streaming down her round face.

"What is it? *What?*" I demanded.

"The . . . the carriage. The jolting." She was weeping. "The bruise is bleeding. He's in terrible pain."

I towed her over to a chair and made her sit down in it. Then I dug in her handbag for a handkerchief and some smelling salts. "Don't cry so, Ania Alexandrovna," I said, kneeling beside her. "The

Tsarina may want you. You must be calm."

"Yes . . . Yes . . . " she gasped. She dabbed at her eyes, but broke down in loud sobs again.

"Won't you rest in your room?" I begged. "They'll send word how he is." At last I managed to persuade her. I settled her on the bed with a cold cloth over her eyes, then sat listening to her weeping. How could Alexei be so ill now? He'd seemed well this morning!

Every five minutes, Ania would send me for news. The Big Pair had joined the Little Pair outside Alexei's room. Olga sat with her arm around Marie, who was weeping, and Anastasia was pacing back and forth, biting her lips. Tatiana stood guard by the door, looking grave. As usual, she was the one who kept her head.

"It's better if Ania stays in her room," I explained to her. "But she won't unless I keep coming for news."

Tatiana nodded. "Do your best to keep her quiet, Dunia," she said. "Mama has enough to worry about without having to deal with Ania just now." She opened the door and slipped inside. Before it closed, I glimpsed Alexandra Feodorovna and Dr. Botkin bending over Alexei's bed. A moment later Tatiana appeared, shaking her head. "Nothing has changed. Dr. Botkin says it is a bad one. But don't tell Ania that," she added.

A bad *what?* I wondered. I found Ania sitting up, her face swollen from weeping. "There's no news," I told her. "Dr. Botkin is there." I knelt down beside the bed. "*Please* tell me what's wrong, Ania Alexandrovna," I said, smoothing back a strand of her hair. "I love him too!"

Her lips trembled. "It's a secret," she faltered. "A state secret, because the Tsarevich is the Tsar's only son. Only he can inherit the throne. You must swear never to tell a soul, Dunia!"

I crossed myself. "I swear before God!"

"Alexei Nikolaevich has a disease," Ania began. "A terrible disease." She gulped back a sob. "If something makes him bleed — a bruise, a little cut, oh, anything — the bleeding won't stop. It goes on and on inside his body, and it . . . it hurts him terribly!" she finished.

"But can't the doctors cure him?" I gasped.

She shook her head. "They can do little. But when our blessed Father Grigory prays over Alexei, God hears him and the bleeding stops."

I sank back on my heels. It all made sense now. That was why Anastasia had been so frightened when she let it slip that Alexei's arm had been bleeding. And why the Tsarina sent secret messages to Grigory begging for his prayers. No wonder he dared to ask her — the Tsarina! — to help him get rid of his enemies! Because only Grigory could save her son's life . . .

But Grigory couldn't really help Alexei, could he? Then I remembered. The field, the cut horse, blood flowing, then stopping . . . I clapped my hand over my mouth. Grigory *could* stop bleeding. I'd seen him do it.

"What is it, Dunia?"

Ania was staring at me. I just shook my head.

"N-nothing, Ania. Poor Alexei — oh, it's horrible!"

"And Father Grigory is in Siberia now," said Ania, wiping her eyes. "This time he can't help. May God have mercy on us all!"

The dark passages of Spala became the scene of a nightmare. Day after day, the bleeding continued, and Alexei's pain grew worse. He began to moan, and then to shriek as the pain seized him. Servants plugged their ears with cotton so they could do their work. The rest of us, heartsick, avoided each other's eyes.

But the real horror was played out in the public rooms of the hunting lodge, for there the family had to act as if nothing was wrong. If the outside world discovered the secret of the Tsarevich's disease, the Tsar's enemies would use it against him, and claim that Alexei could never rule Russia. So the family pretended all was well. Anastasia and Marie actually put on scenes from a play for the guests, but the rest of them were acting too. The Tsar, pale with worry, still took the nobles hunting. The Tsarina, who spent days and nights at Alexei's beside, never sleeping, donned evening dresses and greeted her guests. The Big Pair chatted with the visitors, hiding their sorrow behind bright smiles.

Four days dragged by. Word that the Tsarevich was ill began to spread, and at last medical bulletins were issued, never giving the cause of the illness. Still guests came, and the family struggled to entertain them. I hated those guests. Why didn't they have the sense to stay away?

More doctors arrived from St. Petersburg, but all left Alexei's room shaking their heads. A strange machine called a telegraph was set up in a downstairs room. An operator sat there night and day as the machine chattered out messages that piled up by the bushel basketful. People sent holy icons and prayed for Alexei, but still he grew worse.

One night it seemed that the end had come. Alexei's cries died away to a low moaning, and the doctor sent for Alexandra Feodorovna, who was at dinner. I saw her running toward me down the corridor, holding up the long train of her satin gown in both hands. I flattened myself against the wall as she rushed by me, her eyes staring blindly ahead.

My hands shaking, I put down Ania's dinner tray and tiptoed toward Alexei's room. All his sisters were gathered across the hall. Even Tatiana was weeping, her calm broken down at last. But not Anastasia. Still wearing the servant girl's costume from the play, she was curled up in a wing chair by the window, her fists clenched. She was muttering something under her breath. I moved closer.

"Stop it, God! Stop it, God!" she was saying over and over. She stared up at me, her face white with despair under the foolish frill of the servant's cap. "At least God could let him die and end his suffering," she said.

I knelt before her. "No, no, don't say it!" I cried. "He *must* live — he must!"

She stared at the tears running down my cheeks. "You really love him, don't you?" Then, "You know," she went on, "I used to think you were just a nasty lit-tle schemer, Dunia." She turned back to the window, one arm clutched around her as if her stomach were hurting her. "Oh, what does it matter now?"

She had turned all her sorrow to anger, and now it was eating her up. But tears are God's comfort, my mother used to say. "Why don't you weep like the others?" I whispered.

Anastasia's eyes were dry and burning. "I *can't!*" she said. "I never could. Oh, once when I threw a rock at Tatiana and thought I'd killed her. But never since. Things just . . . They just build up inside me."

"You must cry. You *must*," I said. Then, hardly knowing what I was saying, I went on. "Can't you imagine Alexei's pain? What it must be like to lie there bleeding hour after hour?"

"Stop it!" she moaned, clapping her hands over her ears.

Greatly daring, I pulled her hands away and held them. "Imagine waiting for pain you know will always come again, like an enemy you can't escape. Are you too proud to imagine, Anastasia Nikolaevna? How can you love him if you can't suffer with him?"

She cried out and jerked her hands away. Covering her eyes, she burrowed her face into the wing of the chair. Her shoulders quivered. It was moments later when she lifted her head. Tears were spilling from her eyes. She touched her cheek, gazing at her wet fin-gertips. Then she looked down at me. "You made me cry," she said, wonderingly. Then she burst into wild sobs.

"Forgive me, oh, forgive me," I wept. "I didn't want to say those horrible things to you!" Forgetting who she was, who I was, I hugged her. And I felt her wet cheek press itself against mine, my Anastasia.

When I opened my eyes, Tatiana was looking down at us. She gave me a little nod before she turned away.

"Listen," I said, sitting back on my heels and wiping my eyes. "You must stop now. Crying can be a comfort, Anastasia Nikolaevna. But too much isn't good for you."

She hiccupped and pulled out her handkerchief. "I can't seem to get stopped," she faltered, her eyes still brimming over.

"Oh, you! You never know when to stop!" Marie, her face stained with her own tears, perched on the arm of the chair and stroked Anastasia's hair.

"Is he worse, Marie Nikolaevna?" I asked.

"The doctors fear so. He's being given Communion. Oh, if only Father Grigory were here!"

Yes, if only. But Grigory was far away in Siberia, at Pokrovskoe. It might as well have been on the other side of the world.

A door opened somewhere on the floor below, and for a moment, before it slammed again, I heard a distant chattering sound.

The telegraph!

I gasped. If Grigory knew about Alexei's illness, if he used his power, might it still work?

"What is it, Dunia?" Anastasia's tears had stopped at last.

"If Grigory knew about Alexei he . . . he might be able to help."

"All the way from Siberia? But he doesn't know!"

"The telegraph," I said.

Her eyes widened. "Yes!" she cried, jumping to her feet. "Tatiana must ask Mama at once!"

Tatiana raised her eyebrows when she heard, but said, "What harm can it do to try?" She slipped into Alexei's room and beckoned us inside.

Alexei lay on his side, his left leg drawn up tightly against his chest. His eyes, deeply ringed with black, were rolled up and his face was paper white. Only a low moaning showed that he was still alive. Beside him on the bed, half sitting, half lying, was the Tsarina. Her arm encircled him, and she was touching his hair and his brow with the lightest of kisses, as if trying to put strength into him.

"Dearest Mama," whispered Tatiana, touching her shoulder. "Dunia has had an idea. About Father Grigory. I think you should listen. I'll sit by Alexei for a moment."

Wearily, the Tsarina got to her feet and came over to where Anastasia and I waited near the door. Her eyes were sunken with fatigue, her face drawn. Her red-gold hair was threaded with grey at the temples.

"If you let Grigory know about Alexei, he could pray for him," I said. "And maybe God would hear him, even in Siberia."

"The telegraph, Mama," Anastasia broke in. "Dunia thought of the telegraph."

"He could know in just a few minutes," the Tsarina

murmured, a faint hope dawning in her eyes. "And we could have the comfort of a message from him. Oh, why didn't I think of it sooner?" She hurried over to a table and scribbled a message on a piece of paper. Then she handed it to me, saying, "Run, Dunia! Tell the operator to send this at once to Grigory in Pokrovskoe."

I raced to the telegraph room, and hung over the operator as he sent the message, clicking away at his electric key in a flurry of "dits" and "dahs."

"How long before he answers?" I demanded.

"Who knows, malenkaya," he said, sitting back in his chair. "The message goes swiftly. But there may be no one in the office to receive it."

"I'll wait," I said, sitting down on a stool beside the desk. Two hours passed with no reply. Was Alexei even alive now? I asked myself miserably. Perhaps it had been cruel to raise their hopes. It would be my fault, all mine, if they were to be disappointed.

At last I dozed, but was awakened by the chatter of the electric key as a message came in.

"It's from him," the telegraphist said, writing the message down. He frowned. "It's short, though." He folded the paper and sealed it in an envelope. "You take this to the Tsarina, little sister," he said. "And don't you try to read it on the way!"

I flew up the stairs and along the corridor. What had Grigory said?

They were all in the room with Alexei now. The Tsar was sitting on one side of his pillow with the Tsarina on the other, the girls clustered behind her.

Alexandra Feodorovna tore the envelope from my hand and scanned the message. Her face brightened as if she had glimpsed the very gates of heaven. Her eyes met the Tsar's, and she nodded.

"Bless you, bless you!" she said, stooping to kiss my forehead. "Truly, you are a child of God, just as Grigory said. Now come," she added. "You shall read it to Alexei yourself."

She led me to the Tsarevich's bedside. At the sight of his poor face, wasted by suffering, my throat closed and I had to choke back sobs.

Turning to Anastasia, the Tsarina said, "Speak to him, dear. He always hears your voice."

"Alexei," Anastasia said softly, leaning over and stroking his hair. "Try to listen, Alexei. Dunia's here. She has a message from Father Grigory!"

"Dunia." It was as faint as a sigh. His eyelids fluttered, then he looked up at me, his eyes old with pain. "When I die . . . it won't hurt anymore, will it?" he breathed.

"G-Grigory sends you a message, Alexei Nikolaevich," I faltered. Then, struggling to keep my voice steady, I read it aloud. It said: *God has heard my prayers. The little one will not die. Don't let the doctors bother him too much.*

"Ahhh," sighed Alexei, and his eyelids fluttered closed again.

I looked up and found myself gazing into the blue eyes of the Tsar. "My wife has already blessed you, and I bless you again, Dunia Ivanovna," he said. "Whatever happens now, you have comforted my son."

I crept away to Ania, then, and told her the message.

"God be praised," she cried, clasping her hands. "Father Grigory has saved him again."

And so it seemed, for when the Tsarina emerged from Alexei's room the next morning she was smiling. "The doctors don't see any change yet, but a mother knows," she said triumphantly. "He will get well, thanks to the prayers of our good Grigory."

12

Tsar's Weather

February – September, 1913

Anastasia clawed at her pearl-trimmed headdress. "I hate wearing a *kokoshnik*," she complained. "Shura always sticks the pins straight into my scalp."

She and the other girls were dressed in shining gowns of white silk, with diamond-studded scarlet ribbons across their chests. It was the first time I had seen them looking like real princesses.

That year of 1913, the Romanov family had ruled over Russia for three hundred years. Great celebrations were taking place, and we were back in Petersburg, in the Winter Palace. I had thought the Alexander Palace grand, but the Winter Palace was much grander, with its great halls of marble and malachite, its gold and silver and velvet.

"My kokoshnik's quite comfortable," said Marie, patting it. "If you didn't fidget when Shura was helping you dress, you wouldn't have pins sticking into you, Nastasia."

"There. Is that better?" asked Tatiana, pulling a pin out of Anastasia's hair.

"You look very grand," I said, with a satisfied sigh.

"Grand? Nonsense. My dress is tight and my shoes pinch!" Anastasia flounced into a chair. "How would you like having to stand in a line at stupid receptions, nodding and smiling to a lot of boring people? They simper at us as if we were dolls!" She made a face.

I laughed. "But you *do* look like dolls. *Matryoshka* dolls that fit inside each other, each one smaller than the last!"

"Get up, Nastasia, or you'll wrinkle your dress," warned Tatiana.

"Oh, blow," sighed Anastasia. She got up and balanced on one foot, slowly raising the other out of sight under her skirt. "How *do* you *do*, Princess Snootinski?" she warbled, with a toothy grin. Then she put her foot down and crossed her eyes. "Grrreetings, Your Imperial Boringness," she trilled, wagging her head from side to side.

"*What* are you doing?" asked Olga.

"Practising," said Anastasia.

"You wouldn't!" gasped Marie.

Anastasia grinned wickedly. "I *might!*"

"You'd better not," warned Olga. "If Mama found out she'd never get over it. Anyway, how can we complain? We don't have to go to all the receptions, as Mama does. And she's still worn out from worrying about Alexei."

Anastasia's bright face clouded over, and she turned away. For Spala still lay like a shadow over us.

Alexei had recovered slowly all winter, but still couldn't straighten the leg that had been damaged by the bleeding. To his embarrassment, he had to be carried everywhere in the arms of a Cossack.

"I wish we were back at Tsarskoe," Anastasia groaned, pacing to and fro and rubbing her arms where they emerged from her silken sleeves. "It's gloomy and drafty here."

"So are high cliffs where eagles nest," I said. "But that's part of being an eagle — and the Winter Palace is part of being a Romanov. In my village, people think the Tsars live here all the time."

"Bah! You sound like Grandma Minnie," she said. "She tells Papa and Mama that they owe it to Russia to spend more time in St. Petersburg. But we all like Tsarskoe *much* better."

Marie was primping in front of a mirror. "Do you think Father Grigory will come tonight?" she asked.

I shrugged. Since Spala, the Tsarina had come to meet Grigory several times at Ania's little house, and now he was often in and out of the Winter Palace. I hardly knew what to think of him anymore. Yes, he had saved Alexei. But at times I could hardly bear the sight of him. Like the evil enchanter in a fairy tale, he seemed to be able to be many things at once. The Tsarina only saw the side Grigory chose to show her, the simple starets, the man whose prayers helped Alexei. She never saw the grey wolf, the shapeshifter.

Several times Grigory had sent for me to carry messages to Ania. Always more lists of "enemies" who must be punished, more demands to give a government job to this person, or a fat pension to that one. I wondered how much money he made from it all, for no doubt people paid him well to get favours from the Tsarina. He had put on weight, anyway, and was dressed more richly than ever. But a pig in a gold collar is still a pig.

As always, he sensed my thoughts. The last time he came to Ania's he pinched my arm hard as he was leaving. "You've done well for yourself, my flea," he said, the oily smile he had used in the drawing room vanishing from his lips, and his wolf-eyes narrowing. "Just remember — one word from me in Matushka's ear and you'll be back in Siberia."

Siberia! If I was sent back, I'd end up begging a living until I froze to death, for Big Ivan and my stepmother would never take me back, that I knew. So I watched him play the holy starets and said nothing. The two me's were at war again. The shiny-bright me felt guilty for letting Grigory fool people I loved, but the bad me argued that it wasn't my fault. The newspapers were full of stories about Grigory's drinking and gambling, and they said he used his influence for his own evil purposes. The Tsarina *must* know, I thought. She just didn't want to see what Grigory really was. And I knew why: Grigory *had* helped Alexei. We had all seen it at Spala. So there was no escape for any of us, I told myself gloomily. We were all in his power.

I had seen for myself how angry most people were about Grigory. When the Tsar and Tsarina had attended a thanksgiving service at the great cathedral of Our Lady of Kazan, and Ania and I drove to the church behind the royal carriages, I'd felt the people's disapproval. Dense crowds lined the streets, staring silently at the Tsar and Tsarina. There were smiles when the carriage of the grand duchesses rolled by, with Anastasia gaily waving her handkerchief. But there were no cheers.

"A typical Petersburg crowd," Ania had said bitterly.

As we passed, a man had called out, "Look, there's the Vyrubova, that devil Rasputin's woman!" An angry murmur had run through the crowd, and Ania's cheeks flamed.

No, the people weren't fooled by Grigory, not at all.

But by May at least some people's hearts seemed warmer. The weather was fine and hot after the chilly spring. "Tsar's weather," folk called it. The family travelled around Russia, and outside of Petersburg we didn't hear the muttered complaints. In Holy Moscow, crowds cheered the family. Flags and banners floated on the breeze, and the buildings were decked with flowers. The striped and gilded domes of the Kremlin glittered against the bright blue sky, and the air was full of the booming and clanging of church bells.

"Moscow is better than any fairy tale," I sighed to Anastasia.

"Bah!" she said, kicking off her satin slippers. "People in fairy tales don't get sore feet!"

But, as folk say, every road has two directions. For soon afterward, Alexei fell and bumped his knee and began to bleed. Grigory came and prayed over him, and once more he began to get better. Alone in my room, I wept tears of relief and rage. *Why* did Alexei have to suffer so much? And how *could* God let a man like Grigory have such power? Every time he helped Alexei, his coils tightened around all of us.

As summer blossomed the celebrations waned, and by September they were over. At last we were going to go to Livadia! I could think of nothing else, and peppered everyone with questions. I even dreamed about it.

"All very well for you," complained Alexei. "For me it'll be nothing but hot mud baths!"

"Don't be so grumpy," Anastasia told him. "You know they make your leg better even if they are stinky. Soon you'll be able to run about again."

He heaved a big sigh. "I'm *bored*. I've played all my games and read all my stories."

I took some folded pages out of my pocket. I'd been waiting for just the right moment. "Look, Alexei Nikolaevich. Here's the story you wanted me to write specially for you."

He took it, frowning. "You took long enough about it," he grumbled.

"You said I could take all the time I wanted," I said. "Anyway, I had to get it right."

"A Tale for the Tsarevich," he read aloud. Then, as Anastasia peered over his shoulder, he put his hand over the page. "Go away, Nastasia!" he said. "This is just for me." His lips moved as he silently read the story over. When he got to the end, he looked up, grinning. "It's good! I like the part about the fight with the wolves in the wood. But you know," he added, "you really should dedicate it to me."

"What's 'dedicate'?" I asked.

"Write that it's specially for me. And you should put in my titles."

Anastasia rolled her eyes. "You always fuss about details!"

"I like things to be just right," he insisted.

So I took the title page back, and as he dictated to me I wrote on it: *This story was specially written for His Imperial Highness, the Heir Tsarevich, Sovereign and Grand Duke Alexei Nikolaevich Romanov, by his protégé, Dunia Ivanovna.*

Alexei read it over and nodded. "That's better," he said. "Now people will know it really was for me. I'll keep it with my very best things."

Later, when we were alone, Anastasia said slyly, "You've never made up a story for *me*."

"You never asked me to. Do you want me to write you one?"

She shook her head. "I *hate* reading. I'd rather you told it to me. Make one up about a grand duchess." She curled up in a chair, put her chin in her hands, and gazed at me expectantly.

"You mean right *now*?"

She glanced at the clock. "Why not? *I* have nothing to do until tea-time."

I shrugged, and sat down cross-legged on the floor,

for I never can tell a story sitting in a chair. I pondered for a moment, then began. "Once there was, and twice there wasn't, a grand duchess of Russia. She was known as Her Imperial Uproar, the Grand Duchess Madandbad."

"I'm going to like this," said Anastasia, grinning.

"She was the very *smallest* grand duchess anyone had ever seen . . . "

A cushion whizzed past my ear.

" . . . smaller than a bat, smaller than a bee. Almost, but not quite, smaller than her very good friend, the most worthy Flea . . . "

Anastasia snorted. "How ridiculous. Go on!"

So I told her how Madandbad and the Flea went off to search for a magic soup ladle, because the soup in the palace was tasteless, and how after many adventures, they ended up saving the soup.

The clock struck four and Anastasia bounced out of her chair. "Sometimes I think you're even madder than I am," she said, tweaking my hair as she went by. With her hand on the doorknob, she glanced back. "And you know . . . "

"What?"

"You're right about the soup!" The door slammed behind her.

The white palace of Livadia sat halfway up a mountain, looking down over a rocky beach to the dark blue sea. There were groves of twisted trees with silvery leaves that Ania told me were olives, and black-green trees like columns, called cypresses. Flowering vines rambled over buildings and walls, and there were roses everywhere — pink and yellow, white and red — adding their scent to the smell of the sea.

Oh, what a holiday it was. Even better than the *Standart*. Well, not quite a holiday, for we still had lessons. But even Anastasia couldn't hate lessons outdoors on a marble balcony overlooking the sea. Afterward we walked or drove or clambered down to the beach to swim.

To my delight I quickly learned how, with Anastasia holding my head above water while I kicked, and Alexei shouting orders from the shore. I took to it, and like Alexei's spaniel, Joy, would come out of the water only to shake myself and plunge back in.

One hot afternoon, everyone was up on the beach lazing under striped umbrellas. Alexei had been building a huge sand castle. "I'm really too old for sand castles," he had told me. "This will be my last one, so I'll make it my best."

Anastasia had been helping him, but now the tide was licking at their work, and one turret had collapsed into the waves. Frantically, she scooped a trench in the wet sand around the castle. Her hair hung in strings, and she had torn a great hole in her bathing suit.

Picking up Olga's camera, I called her name. She looked up and I clicked the shutter.

"No fair!" she yelled, jumping up. I dropped the camera and dashed into the water. I got a good way out before she caught up with me and pushed my head under.

"Worth it!" I spluttered when I got back to the surface. "Just wait until you see the picture!"

"I'm going back," she said, treading water beside me.

"I'll just stay a bit longer."

"You'll shrivel up like a pickle!" She struck out for shore.

I rolled onto my back and floated for a few moments, my eyes closed against the blazing sun. Then I bobbed upright. Anastasia was near the beach, and I set out after her. Then, out of nowhere, a huge wave surged under me, lifting me into the air. Up and up I went, the wave carrying me forward. Anastasia was right ahead of me now, and below.

"Look out!" I shouted, just as the crest of the wave broke over her, pulling me under too. Spluttering and coughing, I struggled to the surface. The ebb was pulling me farther from shore. I trod water. Where was Anastasia? Far away on the shore I could see tiny figures running . . .

I took a gulp of air and I plunged under the surface, opening my eyes against the salty sting of the water. I saw nothing, only shafts of sun slanting down. I had to surface. Another gasp of air, another plunge. Still nothing, then . . . something waving like seaweed below me. Anastasia's hair!

My lungs bursting, I kicked deeper and grasped a handful of it. I tried to tow her upward, but, oh, she was heavy, heavy. I saw light glinting on the surface far above me, and knew I'd never reach it. Then that watery sky shattered and another body plunged past me. I felt myself grasped around the waist and carried to the surface.

Coughing and gasping, I opened my eyes. It was the Tsar, with Anastasia under one arm and me under the other. More swimmers had caught up with him now, and one of them seized me, while the Tsar set out for shore towing Anastasia.

People were shouting and running around on the beach. The gentleman-in-waiting who had brought me to shore wrapped a huge towel around me and carried me up to the umbrellas.

A silent crowd had gathered around the Tsar and Anastasia. I struggled free of the towel, pushed through the throng and knelt beside them. Anastasia was lying face down. The Tsar was trying to revive her. "She was under so long," someone in the crowd murmured.

But moments later she gasped and shuddered. Instantly the Tsar turned her over and sat her up. Water gushed from her nose and mouth, and she began to retch.

"God be praised!" said the Tsar, wrapping her tenderly in a towel. He lifted her in his arms and started back up to the palace. "Someone carry the other little one," he called over his shoulder.

And so I was scooped up from where I knelt on the rocky shingle, and carried away, and it was just as well, for I had suddenly begun to shiver and couldn't stop.

That night they let me see Anastasia, though only for a few moments. The Tsar was there, and the

Tsarina. Alexandra Feodorovna got up from Anastasia's bedside and came over to where I stood in the doorway. She stooped and kissed me on the forehead. "Thank you, dear child," she murmured.

"That's right," the Tsar said to Anastasia. "You owe your life to Dunia, you know. It was she I saw bobbing to the surface. When I dove for you there she was, hanging onto you by the hair. Otherwise I'd never have found you."

Anastasia turned her head on the pillow and gazed up at me. She had a great bruise and scrape on her forehead where the wave had dashed her against the bottom. She raised her hand to her hair and frowned, her eyebrows drawing together almost into a line. "Did you have to pull my hair so hard?" she complained. "My whole head hurts!"

But that wasn't what her eyes said, my Anastasia.

13

Ships

November, 1913 – July, 1914

The family lingered on at Livadia through the autumn and winter. The mud baths helped Alexei, and his leg began to straighten. Even the Tsarina seemed happy there, though she was awfully cross with Ania.

Anastasia said it was because the Cow was mooning over the Tsar again. "She keeps hanging around, hoping he'll ask her to go for a walk," she said, shrugging.

I wondered why the Tsarina invited Ania to come at all if she was cross with her.

Anastasia blew a puff of air up under her bangs. "Well, I shouldn't tell you. It's sort of a secret, but . . . You see, a long time ago Ania was in love with a man Mama didn't like, and Mama made her marry Captain Vyrubov instead," she said. "And Captain Vyrubov beat her!"

Beat her! I knew what that was like. No wonder

poor Ania doted on the gentle, kindly Tsar.

"So Mama feels she did Ania a great wrong, and now she tries to look after her, even if Ania is silly sometimes," finished Anastasia. "But don't ever let on I told you."

Of course I wouldn't. I was dying to know what happened to the wicked captain, though. But I didn't like to ask Anastasia to tell more secrets.

The winter days finally passed, and then it was spring, the hillsides pink and white with the blossoms of cherry and almond orchards, the plains a carpet of violets.

"They're my very favourite flower," said Anastasia, plucking great handfuls. "I could just roll in them!" Then she actually did it.

We spent whole afternoons together now, while the Big Pair and Marie were playing tennis. Little by little Anastasia told me some of her secrets — how she thought she wasn't as pretty as her sisters, and how she often felt restless and impatient with everything, and didn't really understand why.

I told her some of my secrets too. When she heard about Big Ivan, Anastasia's blue eyes went stormy, and her brows drew together. "I just wish I'd known you then" she said fiercely, smacking her fist into the palm of her hand. "I'd have told Papa, and he'd have put your father in jail for beating you!"

Tears sprang to my eyes and I had to swallow hard. No one had ever taken my part that way before.

In June, the family made a brief trip to Rumania. The moment they got back Anastasia dragged me into a corner. "I've got another secret!" she whispered. "They were planning to marry Olga off to Crown Prince Carol of Rumania. But Olga said no, so the prince started making eyes at Mashka." She hugged herself with glee. "She'd probably say yes if he asked her. Bow-wow would marry just about anybody. But she's too young, of course. Mama would never allow it."

"Well," I teased, "it will be your turn next."

Anastasia tossed her head. "No fear of that! I don't mean to marry until I'm ever so old. I'm going to have plenty of fun first."

At last it was time to leave Livadia. Soon we were on the deck of the *Standart*, and anchored off the fortress of Kronstadt. A line of British warships steamed slowly past, grey and grim, their turrets bristling with enormous guns.

"At least it's not Uncle Willy this time," said Alexei.

Marie was hanging over the railing. "Look — sailors!" she cried. "And Papa said we may go aboard and visit them."

Anastasia gave me a nudge, and rolled her eyes.

After the naval review, the Tsar invited the British admiral to Tsarskoe. He was very handsome, and Marie talked about him and his sailors for days afterward.

"Honestly, Mashka, with you it's anything in a uniform!" Tatiana sighed.

"Well, thank goodness they've all gone home," said Anastasia. "Now we can go to Finland."

It was Tsar's weather, hot and clear. The family boarded the *Standart* again, chattering about how much cooler it would be at sea. Then Alexei, who was halfway up the ladder, gave a cry of pain. "I've twisted my ankle!" he called up. "Give me a hand, will you?" A young officer clambered down to help him "It's nothing, Mama," Alexei insisted when he reached the deck, for the Tsarina's face had turned chalk white under the brim of her shady hat. But during the night he began to be in pain.

In the morning, we were in Finland again, anchored in the bay of the *Standart*, but no one felt like going ashore.

"He's bleeding inside the ankle joint," I overheard Dr. Botkin tell the Tsar, who was pacing up and down the deck. "It's terribly painful." Alexei screamed from below, and the doctor hurried away. The Tsar leaned his elbows on the railing and buried his face in his hands.

"Mama telegraphed right away to Father Grigory," Anastasia whispered.

So we took to hanging about the ship's telegraph office. Three days after Alexei hurt himself, a message began to come in. The telegraph officer suddenly jerked upright. His lips moving, he wrote down the message. "This goes to the Tsar at once!" he called to his superior officer as he ran past us out the door.

"Do you think that was from Grigory?" I asked.

Anastasia shook her head. "He'd go to Mama, not to Papa. Let's ask Olga this afternoon. Papa always tells her news, if it's not state secrets."

Olga told us that an Austrian archduke had been murdered by a Serb terrorist, and that Austria was threatening to declare war on Serbia.

Anastasia's face fell. "Will we have to go back?" she asked.

"Not yet," said Olga. "Papa will keep in touch with his ministers by telegraph."

How could one archduke be so important? I wondered. After all, there must be lots left. But I didn't say it, in case he was a relative.

We went back to our vigil at the telegraph office. Many messages flew back and forth, then there came one made that made the telegraph officer grin. "Great news!" he exclaimed to his superior. "Someone has stuck a knife in that villain Rasputin. With any luck he's dead by now!"

"Not so loud," warned the other officer, jerking his thumb in our direction. "Run along now, Anastasia Nikolaevna," he added, shutting the door in our faces.

"I must tell Mama!" Anastasia gasped. She turned and ran for her mother's quarters.

I stood frozen to the spot. If Grigory died, I'd be free of his shadow. But what about Alexei?

Grigory did not die, though. We learned that his family took him to Tiumen, and there was an operation. Little by little he began to recover.

"Thank God," breathed the Tsarina, who had spent long hours on her knees praying for him. "Now he is conscious, and will pray for Alexei!"

Whether it was Grigory's prayers or not, Alexei

did improve. The bleeding stopped, though his ankle remained swollen and he had to be carried ashore when we returned to Peterhof.

And now yet another fleet appeared, this one bringing the President of France to our doorstep.

"Not *more* stupid ships!" moaned Anastasia, peering through the telescope from the tower room at Peterhof. "They all have to have visits and receptions and banquets, and Mama gets cross!"

"That's not kind, Nastasia. You know it's only because she gets so terribly tired." Olga sighed.

"But why do they all have to come?" Anastasia asked.

"It's hard to explain about the ships," Olga told her. "It's something about alliances."

"What's an alliance?" I asked.

"It's like a friendship. Two nations say they will be friends and fight each other's enemies."

I nodded. That seemed all right.

"Papa has alliances with France and Serbia," Olga went on, "and Uncle Willy has one with Austria. Remember, it was a Serb who killed that Austrian archduke, and so . . . "

Anastasia frowned. "You mean Papa has to back Serbia, and Uncle Willy has to back Austria?"

Olga nodded. "And if Serbia and Austria get into a war, Papa and Uncle Willy will have to fight each other too. Because nations have to keep their promises, just like people, Papa says."

The French President sailed away at last, but we didn't go on the *Standart* again. It was still hot, terribly hot. It felt as if the world was melting.

One day when Ania returned to the cottage from a visit with the Tsarina, I could see that she had been crying.

"It's Father Grigory," she sighed, sinking into a chair and fanning herself. "He has telegraphed the Tsar and told him not to go to war. Nikolai Alexandrovich is furious! He tore the telegram to pieces and he . . . he spoke quite sharply to me. He said the army is none of Father Grigory's business! I was just relaying Grigory's messages, as the Tsarina has asked me to," she finished, her lower lip trembling.

Poor Ania! But for once what Grigory had done made sense. He said he had to save Russia — and what better thing to save it from than a war? Though I couldn't imagine what a war would be like. The worst I'd seen was two drunken peasants whacking each other with cudgels. Now I remembered the great ugly muzzles of the guns on the warships, and shuddered.

That night I dreamed I was back at Spala, the woods dark and menacing all around me. And a stag burst out of the bushes, with great black dogs, their eyes fiery red, coursing behind it. I saw the eyes of the stag as it fled across the path, and its eyes were the eyes of the Tsar.

The next evening at dinnertime we waited and waited for Nikolai Alexandrovich, the dishes of food growing cold on the sideboard. At last the Tsarina told Tatiana to go and fetch her father, but just then the Tsar came in, his face as pale as ashes.

"I've done everything I can to avoid it, but it is war," he said simply.

"No! Oh, no!" cried the Tsarina. "This is the end. The end of everything!"

We all burst into tears.

14

War

August, 1914 – November, 1915

At first it seemed that the Tsarina was wrong. When people heard that war had been declared, they rushed into the streets to cheer and sing "God Save the Tsar." In St. Petersburg, both the Tsar and Tsarina appeared on the balcony of the Winter Palace. The crowd in the square below chanted, "Batushka, Batushka, lead us to victory!" Then they dropped to their knees and prayed.

"It's wonderful," sighed Ania. "All the strikes have been called off, and the workers are rallying to support the Tsar!"

"Do they want to fight, then?" I asked.

"No," she said. "But they fear Germany. And I'm only afraid . . . " She bit her lip.

"Of what, Ania Alexandrovna?"

"I'm afraid for the Tsarina. She's German — she was a princess of Hesse before she married the Tsar."

"But she's our Matushka now. How could people

blame her for being born German?"

Ania sighed. "Dear Alexandra Feodorovna has never been popular. Just because she likes to live quietly at Tsarskoe, people say she keeps the Tsar away from Petersburg, away from his duties to society. And people are also angry about . . . our friend."

"Grigory?"

Ania nodded. "If only people understood how his prayers stop the Tsarevich from bleeding!"

But how could they understand? The Tsar and Tsarina would never let it be known, since that would mean admitting that Alexei might not be fit to rule Russia. For Alexei's sake, the Tsarina would never desert Grigory, no matter what foolish or wicked things he did. *And he knew it!* That was why he even dared to give advice to the Tsar.

We all pored over the papers to get the latest war news. France and Britain had entered the war on Russia's side. The Tsar swore solemnly never to make peace while a single enemy soldier remained on Russian soil, and Russians went wild with delight. He even changed St. Petersburg, a German name, to Petrograd, a Slav one.

And so our troops marched off to war. At first, good news flew back from the front. In early August, the Russian armies were advancing in eastern Germany and in the Balkans.

"Hooray for Cousin Nikolasha!" cheered Alexei, who was putting pins on a map to mark each victory. For the Grand Duke Nikolai, the Tsar's cousin, was the commander of our army.

But as the weeks went on, I began to realize how huge a thing war really was. It changed everything. Suddenly our lessons and games seemed childish, and we all yearned to do something useful. The Tsarina and the Big Pair and Ania began to train as nurses. Anastasia and Marie begged to train too, but their mother refused.

"An operating room is no place for little girls," she said. "There will be many horrible sights there that I would not want you to see."

"But we're *not* little girls!" Anastasia argued. "Marie is fifteen. Just look how tall she is, and she's as strong as an ox. And I'm thirteen, not a baby. I've grown — well, a bit — since last year, and I'm tough, too! Why can Olga and Tatiana train, if we can't? It's not fair!"

"It's not, Mama," pleaded Marie.

Alexandra Feodorovna shook her head. "Olga is nineteen and Tatiana seventeen. They are grown-up young ladies now. That is different."

"Oh, blow!" muttered Anastasia, plopping down into a chair.

The Tsarina smiled. "I know how badly you want to help. Listen, Nastasia. We are setting up a convalescent hospital in Feodorovsky Gorodok. When the time comes, you and Marie can visit the wounded soldiers there — take them comforts and cheer them up."

And with that the Little Pair had to be content. A hospital was also set up in the Catherine Palace, and once they had finished their training, Alexandra

Feodorovna and the others toiled for long hours helping the doctors in the wards and operating rooms. There was no task too bloody or dirty or frightening for Tatiana, for to no one's surprise, the "governess" turned out to be a wonderful nurse. No matter how tired she got, her face glowed under her starched veil.

"At last I'm doing something that matters," she told Ania. "And I'm making friends!"

With poor Olga it was quite different. One afternoon I found her sitting by a window after she had returned from the hospital. She was white to the lips and tears were rolling down her cheeks.

"What is it, Olga Nikolaevna?" I cried.

"I'm such a c-coward," she sobbed. "Oh, if they'd let me go to the front, I could shoot Germans. But I just can't s-stand seeing those poor men all shot to pieces. There's blood everywhere. And the awful operations — sawing off their arms and legs!" She buried her face in her hands. "I'm always sick to my stomach. I thought I'd get over it, but I haven't. Today I fainted. Oh, I hate myself. Why can't I be strong and brave like Tatiana?"

Anastasia poked her head around the door. "What's the matter with Olga?" she demanded.

"It's the nursing. It makes her awfully sick. She says she's a coward, but of course she isn't."

"She's no coward," said Anastasia, coming over. "She just thinks too much. She reads too many books — I knew it couldn't be good for her!" She stared down at her sister. "See here, Olga," she said. "You can't go on this way. Just look at you. You're going to make yourself sick, and then we'll have to nurse *you!*"

"Must Olga Nikolaevna attend operations?" I asked. "Couldn't she do something else?"

"Why not?" said Anastasia, brightening. "There must be dozens of things she could do!"

"But . . . Mama?" Olga said. "She expects so much of us. She'll be so disappointed in me."

"I'll get Tatiana to speak to her. She'll talk Mama around, just wait and see," said Anastasia.

So Olga was allowed to supervise some of the wards in the hospital. No matter how many new nurses were trained, though, or how many hospitals were set up, there were never enough. For as folk say, a wide road leads to war, but only a narrow path leads home again. By autumn, the Russian armies were losing battles against the Germans, and more and more trains rolled eastward from the front laden with wounded and dying soldiers.

The men in our little hospital were the lucky ones. They had survived the battlefields, and their wounds were healing. But they were lonely and far from home, and glad of our visits.

Anastasia poked her nose into every detail of "her" hospital, asking questions and giving orders. The doctors and nurses put up with her with heroic patience, though I saw them roll their eyes at each other. She was very popular with the patients. "Here comes the little one, the malenkaya," they would say. And she would perch on the edges of their beds and chat away, making up nicknames for them, telling

145

jokes, playing little tricks on them or challenging them to games of checkers.

And I? I was the photographer, and often took and developed snapshots for the soldiers to send home to their families.

In between our hospital visits we still had lessons. We also rolled bandages and knitted socks for the soldiers at the front — though how useful the socks were, I'm not sure. Anastasia's socks, at least. "If the Germans don't kill the poor man who wears this sock," she said, holding up a lumpy grey object skewered on her knitting needles, "the blisters he gets from it probably will!"

"You need to unravel some rows and start over," said Marie. "Here, let me fix it."

Anastasia eyed Marie's flying fingers. "You're wasted as a grand duchess," she snorted. "You're a perfect housewife!"

And so the weeks went on. We had heard nothing of Grigory for some time, then, in November, he telephoned Ania.

"The Tsarina is terribly busy just now," Ania said. "We all are — the nursing, you know. Couldn't whatever it is wait, Father Grigory?"

Standing beside her, I could hear how loudly he banged the receiver down. The moment Ania's back was turned, I danced a little jig. She had actually stood up to him! And Alexei had been well for many months now. Maybe they wouldn't need Grigory anymore. He didn't call again, and I began to hope we were truly free of him.

Christmas came and went, hardly like Christmas at all, with few presents and everyone in uniforms. On January 6 we told our fortunes for the New Year by pouring melted wax onto a tray of snow. Anastasia insisted she knew exactly what each strange shape meant.

"Dunia's is a little box," she announced. "She's going to stuff herself with a box of chocolates."

I blushed. It was true that I'd never got over my weakness for them. "Well, what about yours, then?" I challenged.

She pulled a long face. "Can't you see? It's a big fat man. I'm going to fall in love with General Orlov!"

We shrieked with laughter, for the old general was so stout that he couldn't ride a horse.

A week later, on a freezing cold night, Anastasia telephoned the cottage. Ania had gone to Petrograd to see her parents, so I answered. It was Anastasia, her voice choked and strange. "Dunia?" she said. "Please come. Mama wants you."

The family was gathered in the Tsarina's room. They all looked grave, and Anastasia came over and silently took my hand.

"There has been a train wreck," said the Tsarina. "Ania is badly hurt." She dabbed her eyes with a handkerchief. "They think she is dying. We're going to meet her at the station. Do you want to come with us?"

I nodded dumbly, and tears began to flow down my cheeks.

Poor Ania looked like a broken doll when they

carried her off the train. Her left leg was smashed, and her head covered with blood and bruises. They took her to the palace infirmary where she lay delirious. "Grigory," she moaned. "Forgive me, Grigory! Pray for me!" Soon she sank into unconsciousness.

"He's in Petrograd — he could come right away," said the Tsarina. "I will send for him at once."

Grigory swept in the next day. Looking neither to right or left, he strode over to the bed and took Ania's hand. "Ania!" he called loudly. His fixed his pale eyes on her. Great drops of sweat stood out on his forehead.

I knew that look. I had seen it in the field at Pokrovskoe.

"Leave the woman alone," urged the doctor. "She can't hear you — she's dying!"

But Grigory called her name again, and yet again. And the third time, Ania opened her eyes.

"Now rise," he said, holding her eyes with his. She tried to get up, but couldn't.

"Speak to me, then," he commanded. She murmured his name.

He laid her hand down on the coverlet. "Ahhh," he said, letting out his breath in a ragged sigh. "She will live. But she will always be a cripple."

Ignoring the Tsarina and all the rest of us, he turned on his heel and left as suddenly as he had come. But just outside the door he collapsed. The Tsarina crossed herself as he was carried away. "God forgive me for neglecting him," she murmured. "He is a true saint!"

He's not! the good me wanted to shout. And he had probably faked the faint. But — God had let him help Ania . . . Anyway, after that, Grigory was back in our lives.

Ania stayed in the infirmary for six weeks, complaining every minute. I had to be her hands and her legs, running back and forth between her house and the infirmary. At last she came home, her leg swathed in plaster. She had insisted on returning to her own house, but once there, she complained that the family didn't come to see her often enough.

"Some of them visit every day," I pointed out. "And you know how busy they all are now!"

"The Tsarina doesn't care for me anymore," sighed Ania. "She's angry because the Tsar likes me, I know she is!"

"Oh, *Ania!*"

So she complained, and I scurried about helping her. By summer I was pushing her about in a wheelchair, and she steadily got her strength back, but Grigory's prophecy turned out to be true: Ania never walked again without a crutch.

While I was tending to Ania, the war raged on. In May, the Germans had attacked our army in Poland. We lost, and by the summer of 1915, half our armies were destroyed. We couldn't believe it. Our soldiers were the best in the world, everyone knew that. They should only have to throw their caps at the enemy to beat them!

The newspapers began to print wild rumours. We were losing because our troops were being betrayed from behind their own lines. German spies were at work!

Even worse, the stories hinted, wasn't the Tsarina herself a German? What bad advice might she be whispering in the ear of the Tsar? And what about Rasputin? How had a low, thieving peasant gained such power and influence in Petrograd? What good could be said of a government that allowed such things to happen?

In Moscow, crowds rushed into the streets to destroy anything — or anybody — German they could lay hands on. "Put the German Tsarina away in a convent," people shouted. "Hang Rasputin!"

"*Why* are we losing?" Anastasia demanded of one of the soldiers in "her" hospital. "Our soldiers are brave, aren't they?"

"Very brave, Anastasia Nikolaevna," the man replied. "But what good is bravery without enough guns and munitions and supplies? Without enough trains to move our troops, or even boots for them to march in?"

"But why don't we have all those things?" she asked, when we were alone. "It couldn't be Papa's fault. It just couldn't!"

Our Russia was like a giant in a fairy tale, I thought — mighty in size, but clumsy and helpless before the attacks of its enemies.

As the situation worsened, the Tsar decided that he would take command of the army. Ania told me that his ministers had tried to talk him out of it, but that he wouldn't listen. "Dear Nikolai Alexandrovich feels his generals have let him down," she fretted. "But how can he command the army and run the government too? It's too much for anybody, even a tsar!"

So now the Tsar had to spend most of his time at the Stavka, the army headquarters far to the south of Petrograd. To Alexei's delight, the Tsarina decided that he could stay with his father.

With the Tsar away, it was the Tsarina who consulted the government ministers in his place. "I was terribly nervous at first," she admitted to Ania, "but it's my duty to help Nicky bear his burden. I thank God daily for sending Grigory to help me see what is right for our country!"

Night after night she would write long letters to the Tsar, to send him advice.

"Can I send a letter to Papa along with yours?" Anastasia asked her one evening.

Alexandra Feodorovna looked up from her lap desk, her face flushed and eager. "Write it quickly, Nastasia. I have very important things to tell Papa, and the letter must go at once!"

My heart sank. I knew only too well whose advice was in it.

Despite the shadow of Grigory, there were some bright moments. Alexei too wrote dozens of letters. One addressed to me read:

Dear Protégé!

Greetings from the Stavka. Papa and I review a lot of troops every day. My cat, Zoubrovka, walked on one of Papa's maps and left her paw marks all over

151

it. He was awfully good about it. Everyone says I look very military in my uniform. I practise drills with a wooden rifle.

Papa took me to a field hospital. There were many wounded men, and I was very sorry for them.

My leg doesn't bother me at all.

Respectfully,

Private (Imperial Russian Army)
Alexei Nikolaevich Romanov

But soon after came a desperate telegram. Alexei had caught cold, and his sneezes had brought on a terrible nosebleed. He was being brought home to Tsarskoe Selo.

Alexei was carried up to his room. We all crowded around his bed, and his sad eyes gazed up at us above the blood-soaked bandages that covered his face.

Anastasia squeezed his toes where they made a mound under the covers. "I can't bear it!" she said under her breath. "He has been so well, so happy, for months and months. And now this! Why does God let it happen? *Why?*"

The doctors did everything they could, but the bleeding continued.

"We must send for Grigory," the Tsarina said to Ania at last.

"You want him to come *here*? To the palace?" Ania quavered. "But . . ."

Alexandra Feodorovna's face was set beneath her

white nurse's veil. "I know, I know," she said impatiently. "People will hate me for it. They'll hate you too. But what does that matter, when . . . " She gestured toward Alexei. "And I need the comfort of seeing him," she added.

"Run and telephone him, Dunia," said Ania.

I ran to the nearest telephone, and gave the palace operator Grigory's number in Petrograd. I heard him draw in his breath, so he knew whose number it was. No doubt the news would be all over the palace in minutes.

"Da?" Grigory's voice sounded slurred as it came over the wire.

"Grigory, it's me, Dunia."

"Dunia? Wha . . . What do you want?"

Was he drunk?

"It's Alexei. The Tsarina wants you to come to Tsarskoe at once."

There was a grunt from the other end of the line, and he hung up.

Alexei grew worse. The family were kneeling around his bed when Grigory arrived. He looked as if he hadn't slept for days. His clothes were rumpled, and his eyes had red veins in them. He went over to the bed and stared down at Alexei, then he made the sign of the cross over him. "Don't worry," he mumbled to the Tsarina, who was gazing up at him with pleading eyes. "Nothing will happen."

"Thank God!" she whispered, then, "Won't you stay and pray with us awhile, Grigory?"

He shook his head as if to clear it. Then he turned

and shambled out of the room.

Alexei's eyes closed. The doctor felt for a pulse, then put his hand on Alexei's forehead. "Why, the Tsarevich is sleeping," he said in a wondering voice. "Peacefully sleeping."

15

Plots

January – November, 1916

Until winter fell upon us, wolf cold, our army struggled on, our soldiers fighting for every *verst* of Russian soil they had to give up to the enemy. And still the trains arrived from the front loaded with wounded. The Tsarina got sick and had to give up nursing, and Tatiana struggled to take her place in the operating rooms. Meanwhile, the newspapers openly accused Grigory of interfering with the government, and called Ania an evil influence on the Tsarina.

"But I don't *have* any influence!" protested Ania, looking like a hurt baby. "I only do as the Tsarina tells me. And if Father Grigory wants me to pass requests to her, what can I do?"

"If only Grigory would go back to Pokrovskoe," I sighed.

"But the Tsarina needs him! And the trouble isn't Father Grigory's fault. He's too good to see how unworthy people use him to get favours from the government."

Too *good*? Not Grigory! He could see right through people.

The next time Grigory telephoned, Ania sent me to see him. When I arrived, he looked me up and down. "Well, well. You're getting quite grown up, aren't you?" he said. He squeezed my shoulder, and that strange flicker came and went in his eyes.

I felt as if something had crawled on me, and took a step backward. "What do you want, Grigory?"

"Why, I have more names for you, my flea. Names for Ania to tell Matushka." He grinned. "She knows just when to whisper them to Batushka. Maybe she does it on the pillow at night!"

On Grigory's list, the names Goremykin, Polivanov and Sazonov had rough crosses drawn through them. Below were written three more names: Stürmer, Shuvaiev and Protopopov.

"Time to weed thistles out of the cabbage patch," Grigory went on, scratching himself under his arms. "Those first three have been trying to give me trouble. They'll find out it's a mistake to be my enemy. The last three are fine fellows, and should be put to work right away. Tell Ania to tell that to Matushka."

I copied the list.

"Good, good," said Grigory. "But why such a sour face, my flea?"

"Why don't you leave the Tsarina alone?" I asked. "Don't you see what the newspapers say about you?"

"Why should I leave her alone? *She* doesn't want me to — she begs for my advice." He shrugged. "As for the yapping dogs in the press and the Duma, Matushka must ignore them. They don't understand the Russian soul."

"You don't care about Russia," I burst out. "You only care about yourself!"

His eyes blazed. "God tells me what is good for Russia," he snarled. "Hold your tongue and do as you're bid, if you know what's good for you."

My good self warred with my bad self all the way back to Tsarskoe Selo. If I carried Grigory's messages, I was as bad as he was. But if I didn't, he would tell the Tsarina to send me away! Would she do that? Anastasia and Alexei and the others wouldn't want her to, but she always did what Grigory wanted . . . And if she *did* send me away, where could I go in a country turned upside down by war?

Then I thought of my mother and for a moment I *knew* she was watching me from heaven. She wouldn't want me to do what was wrong . . . I jumped up and threw open the window. Taking a deep breath of cold air, I held the list out. For a moment my wicked fingers wouldn't let go, but I made them give it to the wind. The moment it was done, though, I began to tremble. But, better to eat bread with water than pie with trouble. I sat back down on the seat.

I told Ania I had lost the list.

"Lost it! How *could* you, Dunia?" she groaned. "Can't you at least remember the names?"

I shook my head, though I remembered them very well.

She sighed. "Well, perhaps he'll forget all about it. Sometimes he changes his mind."

I scanned the papers looking for the names of the men Grigory wanted to get rid of, and it didn't take me long to find them. My heart sank, for Goremykin was the prime minister, Polivanov was minister of war, and Sazonov was the foreign minister. Grigory's "enemies" were the highest officials in the Russian government!

And Grigory didn't forget about them. A few days later the telephone rang. Ania's face was white as salt when she hung up. "He wanted to know if I'd given the list to the Tsarina yet," she said. "I had to tell him what happened, and he's furious. Now *I* have to go and get the list."

Heartsick, I waited for her to say Grigory was sending me away, but she didn't. Did he have other plans for me?

So Ania travelled to Petrograd, taking Igor along to help her get around. She returned with Grigory's list.

Two weeks later, the newspaper headlines screamed that Goremykin had been dismissed, and Stürmer was the new prime minister. Before the summer, the rest of Grigory's "enemies" had been destroyed, and his "fine fellows" put in their places. What would happen to Russia now?

By June, Alexei was well enough to return to the Stavka with the Tsar. In July, the rest of us went down to visit them. Alexei was almost twelve now, and looked tall in his uniform as he proudly showed us around. The Stavka was already crowded to bursting with officers, so we lived on the imperial train, which pulled into the forest beyond the station.

While the Tsarina rested in the mornings, OTMA would wander around the village of Mogilev, visiting cottages and playing with the children. At noon, cars would come to take them all to lunch at the Stavka. After lunch, the Tsar would take the children for an hour's tramp across the countryside, returning in time for tea. I looked after them with longing eyes, but Ania became fretful if I left her, so I had to stay behind.

"Guess what?" Anastasia asked when they came back one day. "Olga's in love!"

"In love? Who with?"

"I'll give you a clue: his initials are D. P.!" she said, grinning. "And he's very good-looking!"

"Dimitri Pavlovich?" The handsome young grand duke, one of the girls' cousins, was a great favourite of the Tsar and Tsarina, and he was on the Tsar's staff at the Stavka. "But how do you know?"

"Just watch her," said Anastasia.

So I did. Olga certainly seemed livelier than usual. She blushed a lot, and her eyes followed Dimitri Pavlovich. I couldn't see that he singled her out more than any of the others, though.

Anastasia took it all very seriously. "He'd just better love her back," she said darkly. "Olga will mind terribly if he doesn't."

One blazing afternoon the family was having tea in the garden of the Stavka. The grand duchesses were teasing Dimitri Pavlovich, and the Tsarina was chatting with a group of officers. Ania had gone back to the train with a headache, and I was sitting under the shade of a large lilac bush. Not far away, another knot of officers were smoking and staring at Alexandra Feodorovna.

"Well, here's the Tsarina again," sneered one of them. "Come to give the Tsar the latest orders from her lover Rasputin!"

The words hit me like a blow. How could they say such a filthy thing? The Tsarina would never think of Grigory *that* way! I licked my lips and tasted salt from the sweat on my face.

On and on the officers went. The Tsar was too weak to control the Tsarina . . . She was giving secrets to the Germans, betraying Russia . . .

Why, they were nothing but a nest of vipers! How dare they say such things?

Just then, Anastasia came running across the garden. The officers moved away.

"Marie is in heaven. So many officers — " she began. Then she saw my face. "What's wrong?" she asked. "You've gone all pale."

"It's the heat . . . " I began feebly.

"It is *not*," she snorted. "I know when something's going on." She glanced across the garden at the Tsarina. "Mama's all upset, too. Oh, she smiles and smiles, but she has red blotches all over her face. That always happens when she's nervous. See here," she went on, dropping onto the bench beside me. "It's high time everyone stopped treating me like a baby. Mama and Olga and Tatiana never tell me anything, and I'm tired of it." Then, thumping her fist on her knee, "I'm fifteen now, after all!" Her blue eyes were flashing.

"B-but if *they* won't tell you things, how can I?" I asked, miserably.

"Easily," she snapped. "I'll tell you what I think, and your face will tell me if I'm right. You won't have to say a word." Before I could reply, she rushed on, "I'm not stupid, you know. I have eyes and ears. I can see when Papa is worn out and worried, and when Mama is frightened. Things are going wrong in Russia, aren't they? And not just the war, either."

I looked down at my lap.

"I thought so. People hate Mama for being born a German. I *know* that. It's stupid. She's more Russian than any of us now." She sighed. "But it's troubles with the workers and the Duma, too, isn't it?"

I stared at her in surprise, for never had I heard her talk about such things before.

"Oh, yes," she nodded. "Dunce that I am, I still look at the newspapers — when I can steal them. The others try to keep them from me, you know." She made a face.

Thanks be to God the newspapers hadn't dared to report the scandal about the Tsarina and Grigory, I thought. At least Anastasia was spared knowing that!

"So Mama's upset these days, and Ania's always

bursting into tears. And the newspapers say nasty things about Papa's government." She flushed. "They even say that maybe the Romanovs have ruled Russia long enough! And they print horrible lies about Father Grigory, too. He can't do the things they say he does," she insisted. "He's a good man — look how he helps Alexei!"

I wiped my face on my sleeve. I didn't want to fool her, but how could I tell her what Grigory really was? How could I tell anybody?

"Anyway, I'm going to go and tell these officers they better get busy and win the war. Then Papa can fix what's wrong with Russia," she announced. "Now, come and have a glass of lemonade before you melt," she added, jumping up.

As I trailed after her, I was remembering what Jim had said so long ago. Would the Tsar have time to win the war before the pot boiled over?

Summer faded and autumn came, and still the war dragged on with no end in sight. One morning, Ania was called to the palace. She came back pale and trembling. "What is it, Ania?" I asked, jumping up from the pile of snapshots I had been sorting.

"One of the Tsar's uncles has written a horrible letter to him," she sighed, sinking into a chair. "He accuses the Tsarina of treason, of supporting the Germans. He says she's a tool of Father Grigory. The Tsar's relatives are demanding that he lock her up until the war is over."

Even the Tsar's family was afraid of Grigory!

Ania dabbed at her eyes with her handkerchief.

"The letter says that if the Tsar doesn't act, murders will begin."

"Murders!"

Ania nodded. "And . . . and they mean me too. They blame me for speaking for Father Grigory to the Tsarina. Oh, Dunia, I'm afraid!" she whimpered.

"Don't cry, Ania Alexandrovna. The Tsarina will protect you," I murmured, stroking her arm.

"But she herself is in danger, don't you see?" wept Ania. "There are plots everywhere!"

My heart was heavy. Had I not helped to bring this sorrow and danger to my dear ones? And even though I knew what kind of man Grigory was, wasn't I still his creature?

16

Messages

November – December, 1916

Despite her fears, Ania still went to Petrograd to see Grigory. One day she returned from the city with a bundle of black and brown fur tucked into her coat pocket.

"What is it?" I asked, as it skittered about the polished floor.

"A King Charles spaniel," Ania explained. "For Anastasia. She doesn't have a pet."

Anastasia was thrilled. "Isn't he sweet?" she asked, cuddling him.

I shrugged. "He looks like a *suslik*," I said, for he was exactly like one of those bushy-tailed rodents.

She scowled. "He does not — he's lovely! I'm going to call him Jimmy."

After that she carried him everywhere, for he was too small even to climb stairs. She spent hours teaching him tricks, and one day she invited me to a special performance. Dressed up in a little hat and skirt, the suslik pranced on his hind legs and turned around and around. I clapped, but my heart wasn't in it.

"I can't make you laugh anymore," Anastasia complained, flopping down on the sofa beside me. "You're awfully glum. What's the matter with you?"

"It's Grigory," I told her. For though I tried not to think about him, I knew in my heart that throwing the list away was not enough. I had to tell someone what I knew. Not Ania, for she'd never believe me. And if not her, who?

Anastasia sighed. "You know Mama doesn't like us to talk about Father Grigory."

"I know, Anastasia Nikolaevna."

"I will, though, if you want me to," she said, with a sideways glance under her lashes. "We know Father Grigory is good, but he seems to have a lot of enemies. Is that what's worrying you?"

I nodded. It was, in a way. I knew Grigory's enemies were right. But how could I say that to Anastasia? The Tsarina had taught them all to trust him completely.

She patted my cheek. "You're getting awfully like Olga, you know. Brooding over everything. But if it's about Father Grigory, you should speak to Mama."

"I'd never dare," I gasped. For though the Tsarina was always kind to me, I was still in awe of her. How could I ever tell her what I knew?

"Nonsense!" said Anastasia, jumping up. "I'll ask her this very minute!" Before I could stop her she bolted out of the room and clattered downstairs. Moments later, she reappeared. "Come on," she said,

165

beckoning. "Mama's resting, but she'll talk to you."

She led me down to the Tsarina's lilac-coloured room. "Go away, Isa," Anastasia told the lady-in-waiting on duty. "Mama wants to talk to Dunia."

The Tsarina was propped up on her sofa. She looked pale and ill, but she greeted me kindly. "Little Dunia," she said, holding out her hand. "Come, sit down." Then, "Off with you, malenkaya," she added to Anastasia, who was hovering nearby. "Let Dunia talk to me alone."

Anastasia groaned loudly, but she went.

"Now," said the Tsarina. "Tell me what's troubling you." She smiled. "You're much too young to have big worries."

"It's . . . It's Grigory," I faltered. "There are things about him you don't know."

She raised her eyebrows. "I doubt that. I know what's in the newspapers, Dunia. And I also know that anyone — *anyone* — we are fond of will be lied about and hated."

"But . . . But what they say about him is true!" I burst out. "He's not . . . not always holy the way he is when he's with you. He drinks vodka, and gambles. And he . . . He goes with women," I added, flushing. "It's true. I've seen him, Alexandra Feodorovna!"

The Tsarina's grey eyes were grave. "It must hurt you to speak so about one who has befriended you, Dunia," she said. "You must love us all very much to say these things to me."

I nodded, my eyes brimming with tears.

"Do you think I don't know Father Grigory is not

perfect?" she went on. "He is a simple peasant, after all, as you are. He is the first to admit that he's a sinner, and that sometimes evil people lead him into temptation. But that doesn't mean God doesn't speak and act through him. You know He does, Dunia. You were there at Spala, and the other times."

"But . . . " How could I explain what Grigory really was? I scarcely knew myself. A peasant, yes, but more — a trickster, a shape-shifter, a wild wolf always hungry . . .

Alexandra Feodorovna put her finger to her lips. "Hush. Not a word more. Thank you for telling me what you thought I didn't know. When you are older, you will understand why Grigory's advice is so important to me, and you'll learn to forgive his faults, as I do. Now . . . " She made a little shooing motion with her hand.

I got up and crept away.

I went back to the newspapers, afraid to read more, and afraid not to. A winter as bitter as last year's had set in, and flour and fuel were scarce in Petrograd. People blamed the Tsar's government. What else could be blamed, after all, except the war itself? The Duma was in an uproar over Grigory, and although the politicians never mentioned the Tsarina by name, they hurled abuse at "evil powers close to the Throne." The papers also reported that people still gave parties, with rich food and drink, and ladies in jewels and fancy dresses. They must be mad, I thought, to flaunt their wealth when so many were suffering.

The Tsar was always with the army now, yet one day in late November the whole palace sprang to life, as it always did when he returned.

"It's Prince Carol of Rumania," explained Anastasia. "He's coming on a state visit, so of course Papa has had to come back from the Stavka."

"Isn't he the prince who — ?"

She nodded, grinning. "Mashka's admirer. And she's in a tizzy. She's going to the state dinner for the prince. It's her first formal appearance in society."

On the night of the dinner, OTMA gathered in the Little Pair's bedroom. For the first time, Marie's hair was piled up on top of her head. She was dressed in a gown of palest blue, with high-heeled satin slippers dyed to match. Around her neck sparkled a pearl and diamond necklace, a gift from the Tsar and Tsarina on her sixteenth birthday.

"Do I look all right?" she asked, smoothing her long kid gloves, her huge eyes full of worry.

Olga and Tatiana, dressed in white and pink, exchanged glances, smiling. "Absolutely lovely," said Tatiana. Olga nodded agreement.

"You smell like a garden," I said, sniffing, for each of them was wearing her favourite perfume — Olga's was tea rose, Tatiana's, jasmine, and Marie's, lilac.

"Mine's the best of all," insisted Anastasia, thrusting her wrist under my nose.

There was a strong odour of violets. I sneezed. "Whuff," I said. "You put a lot on!"

She grinned. "Anyway," she said, "why make such a fuss about Mashka meeting the prince? He already knows what she looks like!"

"You're just jealous because you're too young to come too," said Marie. "Oh, these high heels do feel funny," she added, taking a few wobbly steps.

They trailed downstairs in their finery. "Come on," said Anastasia. "Let's watch them go in to dinner!" We hurried across the palace and hung over a gilded railing, looking down into the main hall. Below, footmen were swinging the tall doors of the state dining room open. Silver and crystal glistened down the length of the long table, and chandeliers blazed with candles.

"Here they come!" whispered Anastasia. Below us, the Tsar appeared, leading a richly dressed lady. The Tsarina followed with Prince Carol. Other guests filed after them into the dining room. Then, last of all, came the grand duchesses, each on the arm of a grand duke.

"They *do* look lovely!" breathed Anastasia. Suddenly her eyes were full of tears.

"What's the matter?" I asked.

"Oh, nothing," she replied, rubbing her eyes on her sleeve. "It's just . . . They're all grown up now, you see. It's the Big Trio now, and no one to be with me anymore."

"There's me," I said.

She squeezed my arm. Then, "Look, here comes Mashka," she said. And there she was, floating along with her head held high, every bit as graceful as her sisters. But just as she entered the dining hall, she slipped on the polished wooden floor. Both feet went out from under her, and she sat down hard.

There was a moment of ghastly silence, followed by a roar of laughter from the other guests.

"Oh, poor Bow-wow!" gasped Anastasia, as Marie's grand duke quickly helped her to her feet. "And in front of Prince Carol too!"

Afterward, Marie was in despair. "I'll never live it down, never!" she wept into her pillow. "I can't appear in society ever again. I'll have to become a nun like Aunt Ella!"

"Oh, don't be such an idiot!" said Anastasia, who was perched on the bed handing over handkerchiefs as Marie used them up.

"Nastasia is right," said Tatiana. "People are bound to chatter for awhile, but a year from now no one will even remember it happened!"

"Of course they won't," said Olga. "So stop crying, Mashka. You don't want Prince Carol to see you all puffy-eyed tomorrow."

Marie pulled the pillow over her head. "Prince Carol!" she groaned. "I don't even want to think about *him*."

But apparently the prince didn't mind Marie's mishap, for the next day the Tsar told her that the prince had asked for her hand in marriage.

"He *did?*" cried Marie, reviving like a flower in the rain. "Oh, Papa, what did you say?"

"I told him you were just a schoolgirl," replied the Tsar, his eyes twinkling. It was good to see him smile — he hadn't for many months.

"Papa! You didn't!" cried Marie, horrified.

He ruffled her hair. "Don't be in too much of a hurry to grow up, my Mashka," he said. "If Prince Carol is as fine a fellow as he seems to be, he won't mind waiting a year or two."

"Do you think he *will* wait?" Marie asked us, after the Tsar had gone back to his study.

"I guess he'll have to, if he wants to marry one of us," snorted Anastasia. "He's already had a try for Olga, and he can hardly go back to Tatiana now that he's asked for you." Then she added, "And if he asks me, I swear I'll say no!"

In late December, the Tsarina sent Ania to Petrograd again to see Grigory.

"Do . . . Do you think it's wise?" faltered Ania. "You know what people will say!"

The Tsarina tossed her head. "They say it anyway, whether we see Grigory or not. And it comforts me to have his blessing for Alexei."

"Couldn't I just telephone?" whimpered Ania. "Or send Dunia?"

"I asked you to go in person, Ania," said the Tsarina, raising her eyebrows. "I want to know how he looks, what he's thinking. Take Dunia along to help you get around," she added.

And so we went. A car with the imperial coat of arms drove us through the snowy streets of Petrograd. The city looked as the newspapers had described it — dark and dreary, with lineups outside the shops. Many were shuttered and empty.

The sight of us getting out of the car drew hard

stares from people in the street.

"Look, the imperial coat of arms. Is it the Tsarina?"

"No, it's the Vyrubova!"

"On another mission to Rasputin. Hasn't she done enough harm already?"

Ania shrank inside her heavy furs.

For once there were no people on the stairway to Grigory's apartment. Ania had left her crutch in the car. Leaning on me, she made her way painfully up the stairs.

Grigory was dressed up in an embroidered silk tunic with a tasselled cord around his waist. His velvet breeches puffed out of polished boots. He had even combed the food bits out of his beard. "I'm going to see the prettiest lady in Petrograd tonight," he told us, rubbing his hands gleefully. "The Princess Irina Yusupova. Her husband, Prince Felix, has invited me to meet her, because she isn't well. He feels I can help her. And I *do* like helping pretty ladies!"

"You should keep away from the nobles, Father Grigory" protested Ania. "They hate you, every one of them!"

He smirked. "What if they do? They will not harm me. They fear me too much."

I thought of my innocent ones who believed in him, and how he was betraying their trust. "Why don't you go home to Siberia, Grigory!" I exclaimed.

His eyes narrowed. "I'll go when I'm ready," he snarled. "And when I do, I'll take you with me and drop you on the dung-heap!" Then, as suddenly as it had appeared, the fierce glare vanished from his eyes.

He looked like no more than a dressed-up old peasant. "What do the two of you want?" he asked.

"The Tsarina sent me," said Ania. "She wants your blessing for all of them, but especially for the Tsarevich."

He frowned. "Ah, that Matushka. She's always after me for this, for that," he grumbled. "Sends me all this," he added, waving his hand at the baskets of fruit and flowers that sat on every table. "What good are such things to me?" For a moment he seemed to stare not at us but through us. "What more do you want of me?" he asked in a strange hollow voice. "Already you have received all."

What did he mean?

"Is . . . Is that your only message for the Tsarina?" asked Ania.

He shrugged, and turned his back on us, scratching himself.

Ania began to weep as we went back down the stairs.

"Look! The Vyrubova is crying," an urchin shouted as I helped Ania into the car.

"Wouldn't Rasputin give you any kisses today?" jeered a young woman.

I gazed into the faces of the crowd, pinched and worn by the cruel winter, and saw the depth of their rage and despair. "God be with you," I mumbled, crossing myself. Then the car pulled away and we left them behind.

The next morning, Grigory's daughter Marochka called. "Papa has disappeared," she sobbed. "He went out very late, all dressed up, but he hasn't come back."

When I gave Ania the message, her face turned as pale as cheese.

The Tsarina crossed herself when she heard the news. "Pray God he is only detained somewhere," she said.

But the day wore away and the police could find no trace of Grigory. Someone reported hearing a shot at the Yusupov palace in the early hours of the morning. Prince Felix assured the police that it was nothing. Someone had shot a dog, he told them.

After dinner, I found OTMA clustered on a sofa in the Big Pair's room. It was as if they needed to be close, touching.

"Any news?" asked Olga, looking up eagerly.

I shook my head.

Tatiana's face was solemn. "We are praying that he is all right," she said. "Mama depends so on Father Grigory."

Olga shivered. "I feel cold, cold," she murmured. Marie leaned her head on Olga's shoulder, and Anastasia snuggled close.

I sat at Anastasia's feet and leaned my head against her knee. Then I spoke into the silence. "Once, beyond the thrice ninth land, in the thrice tenth tsardom . . . " And I told them the story of the white duck and the water of life, hoping to comfort them, because I loved them. And because I was afraid for us all. "As it was said, it was done. They all rejoiced, and began to forget the evil days," I finished. And light as the touch of a moth's wing, I felt Anastasia's hand on my hair.

"Thank you," she murmured.

It was past midnight before Ania and I went home to our cottage. "What's happening!" she gasped, as we came out of the woods. For the house was lit up, and we could see dark figures moving about.

A man in a police uniform loomed up out of the darkness. "Are you Ania Alexandrovna Vyrubova?" he asked.

"Y-yes."

"We are here to protect you, gospozha," he said, touching his cap. "We have discovered a plot to kill you and the Tsarina."

With a little moan, Ania slumped to the ground in a faint. The policeman carried her to the cottage, while I ran ahead for the smelling salts.

I sat with Ania until she fell asleep, then went to my own bed. Hours later I woke, as if summoned. Moonlight, white as milk, poured though the window, falling on the portrait of Grigory that Ania always made me keep in my room. Before my very eyes, it fell from the wall and landed on the floor with a crash. The splintered glass caught the moonlight, and for a moment Grigory's eyes seemed to gaze into mine. Suddenly my ears were filled with a dreadful sound — the rumble of angry voices and the tramp of many feet coming nearer and nearer.

Something terrible has happened! I thought. I jumped out of bed and ran to the window. Throwing the casements wide, I leaned out into the icy air, lis-

tening. All was silver silence under the moon. I
closed the window again, and crossed myself, shivering.

17

Shadowland

January – March, 1917

They found Grigory's body two days later, under the ice of the Neva River. A *dog's death for a dog*, the newspapers reported. In Petrograd people kissed each other and some danced in the streets.

At Tsarskoe there was silent despair. The Tsarina spent hours in prayer. Olga looked like a ghost of herself, for one of the men accused of the murder, along with Felix Yusupov, was Dimitri Pavlovich. "It's so hard," she whispered. "All the time he was with us he must have been planning it. *All the time!*"

Ania had Grigory buried under a chapel she was having built in a corner of the palace park. The family gathered, all in black. After the service, the Tsarina gave us each a flower to cast into the grave. The diamond glitter of the sun on the snow made my eyes smart, but I would not weep for Grigory.

The day after the funeral, Ania and I moved into the palace, for the Tsarina feared for Ania's safety. We had rooms not far from OTMA's. I had no lessons now, for dear old Petrov was ill in Petrograd, but Olga brought me newspapers from the Tsarina's reading table.

The news was grim. Terrible snowstorms had blocked the railways, and supply trains couldn't move. Petrograd was locked in a black frost, with little coal for heat and no flour for bread. People scratched a living somehow, and blamed the Tsar, saying he and his government could do nothing right. The politicians in the Duma demanded that the Tsar give Russia a constitution.

Anastasia defended her father. "Papa says we must win the war first. He says we can't desert our allies. Oh, I hate politics!" she added, punching a cushion. "Papa is getting so tired and ill." For the Tsar looked thin and sad now, as though the heart had gone out of him. Our Batushka was doing his best, but it wasn't enough.

One day, Tatiana returned early from the hospital. "They've sent me home," she said, slowly pulling off her starched veil. "The other nurses complained. They don't want to work with the Tsar's daughter." Her eyes filled with tears. "I thought they *liked* me."

"It's not fair!" cried Anastasia, hugging her fiercely. "You've worked harder than any of them!"

In March, the generals asked the Tsar to go back to the Stavka, saying there was danger that the army might mutiny. No sooner had he gone than strikes broke out in Petrograd. The workers cried out for bread to feed their families. They shut down the factories and took to the streets. The newspapers said more than two hundred thousand people were protesting, and the police arrested many of them. The pot was beginning to boil over.

Then Alexei began to complain that his head ached. He was running a fever, and Dr. Botkin said he had measles. "And any of you who haven't had them soon will," he added.

Ania turned pale. "I . . . I haven't had measles," she faltered. "And I do have a headache . . . "

Within hours she was in bed with a raging fever, and Olga and Tatiana too. Then it was Anastasia's turn to fall ill. The Tsarina put on her nurse's uniform and went from one patient to the other, with Marie at her heels. Ania took most of my time. I smoothed her pillows, and made her sip the medicines the doctor prescribed. She was terribly sick, and made herself worse by fretting that the Tsarina was neglecting her.

"But she was here not an hour ago," I told her, smoothing her coverlet.

"Poor old Cow," Anastasia managed to whisper, when I crept in to see her for a moment. "Trust her to come down with a children's disease!"

The sick ones had to lie in darkened rooms, for the disease made their eyes sensitive to light. So the rest of us lived in a shadowland, neither day nor night, falling asleep on sofas or in chairs when we could, then dragging ourselves back to our patients. Their sufferings were dreadful, first burning fever and headache, then piercing pains in their ears.

"I . . . I can't hear you, Dunia!" Anastasia whispered one day, her eyes frightened.

"What's wrong with her?" I cried to Dr. Botkin, who had come up behind me.

"Her ears are filled with pus," he said wearily.

Tatiana suffered in the same way. Olga and Ania were wracked with painful coughs.

"I can't get sick, I just can't," muttered Marie, dropping into a chair for a moment's rest.

Even in the dim light, I could see the black circles under her eyes, and she was terribly thin now. "You must try to sleep, Marie Nikolaevna," I said. "Or you surely *will* get sick."

As the rash broke out on Olga, Tatiana and Ania, their cruel fever broke at last. Alexei, the first to feel better, often curled up on one of his sister's beds to sleep the afternoon away.

The moment Olga began to improve, she wanted to know what was in the papers. She still couldn't read, so I would scan the headlines and report to her when I could.

"The violence is getting worse, isn't it?" she asked, moving her head restlessly on the pillow.

I nodded. Even the armaments factories were closing. They had no more fuel or raw materials. That meant that the war couldn't be fought much longer. And it sent more hungry unemployed people onto the streets of Petrograd.

"I wish Papa hadn't gone to the Stavka," Olga sighed. "I know Mama sees the government ministers while he is away, but she has all of us to nurse . . . "

I said nothing. For I had seen those ministers leave

the Tsarina, shaking their heads.

"It is only hooligans causing the trouble," the Tsarina told Ania, tight-lipped. "Our government policies are right. I tell Nicky he must hold firm. The police just have to keep order. We have a war to fight, and Russia isn't ready for a constitution. Reform must wait!"

But folk say that he who refuses milk to the cat ends by giving the mouse cream. And so it was now. The more people the police arrested, the more went into the streets to protest against the government. People became angrier and angrier. Reform was no longer enough, they cried. The Tsar and his government had to go. It was revolution. Panic spread in the city, as people accused the Tsar of starving the people on purpose. Soldiers and sailors murdered their officers and joined the striking workers. Like the ice breaking up on a river in spring, the violence swept all before it. I remembered the tramp of unseen feet I had heard that December night. Those footsteps echoed now on the pavements of Petrograd.

Suddenly the newspapers stopped coming. We had one last telegram: the Tsar was on his way back, but his train had been stopped and sent to Pskov. Then we heard nothing more. In our shadowland, we could only wait and pray. In the Tsarina's room the last bouquet of lilacs withered, sending out a dying breath of sweetness.

Frightened servants whispered of rioting in the town, and we began to hear bursts of gunfire in the distance. Cossack patrols reported that the soldiers at

Tsarskoe Selo had mutinied, and were marching to capture the Tsarina and Tsarevich. I shuddered when I heard that. A mob, as strong as water, as stupid as a pig . . . They cut the electricity lines, plunging us into darkness.

But loyal troops still surrounded the palace. The Tsarina and Marie went down to talk to them and arrange for shifts of them to come inside to warm themselves. From the window I saw the soldiers braced for a sudden attack. One line was kneeling in the snow, rifles at the ready, with another line standing behind them. The figures of the Tsarina and Marie flitted down the lines, like shadows against the snow.

Perhaps the revolutionaries learned of the troops' readiness, for the attack never came. But two days later, our soldiers were ordered to Petrograd. Our hearts sank as they marched away, flags flying and drums beating. Now we were truly alone.

Soon after that, on a day of howling wind and flying snow, the Grand Duke Pavl arrived and went straight to the Tsarina.

Later, Marie came to find me, her eyes swollen with weeping. "It's Papa," she whispered. "He . . . He has abdicated. Uncle Pavl told Mama the army generals begged him to do it."

Abdicated? Her face told me what the word meant. "He . . . He has given up being tsar?"

She nodded. "Mama cried terribly," she went on. "She's not going to tell the others yet, because they're not well enough."

And so we added lies to the other sorrows of shadowland.

"What's wrong with Mama?" Olga wanted to know. For that day she first heard of the abdication, the Tsarina looked like a dead person walking.

"Her . . . Her heart is bothering her," I faltered.

"What? What?" called Tatiana from the next bed, for she still could not hear. "Write it down for me."

So I took paper and pencil and wrote the lie.

Anastasia lay in a stupor, her fever still high and spots just beginning to appear on her face. At least I didn't have to lie to her, I told myself. Sick at heart, I huddled on the floor beside her bed, and pressed her hot hand to my cheek. I must have fallen asleep, for when I woke, the Tsarina was there.

"Faithful heart," she murmured, touching my hair with the tips of her fingers.

A day later, Marie fell ill. "Who will help Mama now?" she wailed. Soon she slipped into delirium, and raved about "Crowds of dreadful people . . . coming to kill Mama!"

Now I became the Tsarina's arms and legs, helping her nurse the sick, and running her errands. Another day passed, and then at last the telephone rang. Alexandra Feodorovna looked up frowning when a footman burst into the girls' sickroom without knocking.

"Your Imperial Majesty!" he cried. "It is the Tsar!"

"Nicky!" she gasped. Dropping the tray she was holding, she ran out of the room. A few minutes later, she returned, and for the first time in days her eyes looked alive. "He is well. He's coming back," she said. "Tomorrow!"

Then, as she gazed at her daughters, the light in her eyes faded. I knew she was thinking: Now I will have to tell them! I slipped out of the room and closed the door behind me.

"You knew all along, didn't you?" Anastasia whispered later.

"Yes. But your mother didn't want any of you to know. You were too sick."

"I d-don't mind for myself," she faltered. "Or for the others, except maybe Alexei. But poor Papa — he loves Russia even more than he loves all of us! What will happen to him now?" Her lips trembled, and she turned her head away to hide her tears.

"Don't cry," I whispered, smoothing her hair. "Don't cry."

"It's your fault," she sobbed. "You taught me to do it!"

Later that day a general arrived to see the Tsarina. Soldiers surrounded the palace, and began closing up the doors. The general had the rest of us assembled. "The Tsar and Tsarina will be placed under arrest for their own protection," he announced. "Those who wish to leave may leave. Those who stay must stay for good."

People began to slink away. Many who had fed well off the Tsar's bounty were eager to abandon him now. Yet some stayed — Zhilik, Dr. Botkin, the sailor Nagorny, who looked after Alexei, two ladies-in-waiting, and others from cooks to chambermaids. At four o'clock the main doors to the palace were closed, and we were prisoners.

18

Echoes

March – August, 1917

The next morning, the Tsar's train reached the village station. Soon a car drew up before the palace, and the rough-looking soldiers who were our new palace guard threw open the doors. And so he came home to us, our Tsar. For a tsar is anointed with sacred oil when he is crowned, and whatever titles he gives up in this world, he cannot stop being what he is. His face was pale and lined, and his eyes had shadows as dark as bruises under them. He was dressed, as always, in a plain colonel's uniform. He saluted the soldiers, who didn't salute back. Then he shook hands with the few members of his staff who still remained, and disappeared into the Tsarina's rooms.

Later, Alexandra Feodorovna came to see Ania. We heard shouts from outside, and the Tsarina and I hurried to the window.

There below us was the Tsar, surrounded by six soldiers with bayonets fixed on their rifles. "No, you can't go that way, Mr. Colonel," one shouted, nudging him with his rifle. "Stand back when you are commanded!" ordered another, pushing him with his fist. The Tsar turned and walked slowly back to the palace.

"Dear God," said the Tsarina, pressing her hand to her heart.

Oh, Matushka, I thought. You helped bring him to this. You and Grigory and Ania. And I.

That night, Alexei came and sat on the edge of Anastasia's bed. "I'm not going to be tsar," he told me, with a sideways glance. His cheeks were flushed.

"No, Alexei Nikolaevich," I said.

"Papa *did* want me to be," he went on, twisting a corner of Anastasia's sheet into a knot. "But he thought, because of . . . *you* know, Dunia."

His illness, he meant. I nodded. "But Alexei Nikolaevich, your whole family may be going away somewhere out of Russia." For I had heard whispers that they would be sent to Murmansk, where a British warship would pick them up and take them to exile in England. "And if you were tsar you'd have had to stay behind without them."

"You know you wouldn't have liked that, Alexei," Anastasia put in.

"No," he admitted. "And Papa thought that Uncle Misha could be tsar instead. But now he has abdicated too. So what I want to know is, who *is* going to be the new tsar?"

"Maybe no one," I said.

Now we all had to learn how to live again, carefully, carefully, for there was much that was not allowed, and soldiers were everywhere, strolling in and out of the rooms and standing in the dining room at meal times. They searched our supplies, ripping open tubes of toothpaste and stirring jars of yoghurt with their fingers. Alexei grieved because they shot the tame deer and the swans.

One day in March, a man named Kerensky appeared. Olga said he belonged to the new Provisional Government. He was a foxy-looking fellow with reddish hair and green eyes.

Ania turned pale when she heard he had come. Seizing the box in which she kept her letters, she emptied it into the little tiled stove in the corner.

"Strike a match!" she told me. The letters went up in smoke and she threw in more. Soon the stove was clogged with ashes.

There was a pounding on the door. Ania dived into bed and pulled the covers up to her chin. I opened the door, and there was Kerensky. His eyes went at once to the stove.

"I wish to speak with Madame Vyrubova," he said, pushing past me.

"You are under arrest," he told Ania. "Pack your things and prepare to leave the palace at once. I have orders to escort you to the Fortress of Pyotr and Pavl. You are under investigation as an enemy of the people."

Ania shrank down under the covers. "I'm too sick to be moved," she quavered.

"I shall ask the doctors about that," he snapped.

Turning on his heel, he left the room.

"The Fortress of Pyotr and Pavl! They'll murder me there!" wailed Ania.

The doctors said Ania was fit to travel, so Kerensky gave her half an hour to pack. Instead, she sat down on the bed and cried. So I packed what I thought she would need most, and put some of my own things in too. My heart was heavy, but how could I let poor Ania go alone?

When she went to say goodbye to the Tsarina, I slipped upstairs to Anastasia.

"What's wrong?" she demanded, sitting up in bed.

"It's Ania," I said. "They've arrested her."

"But why?" she asked. "Because of Father Grigory?"

I nodded. Out of my pocket, I pulled the snapshot of Anastasia that I had taken on the beach the day she had nearly drowned. I always carried it with me now. "Here," I said, holding it out.

She took it, her eyes widening. "You're going too, aren't you?" she whispered.

"I . . . I must," I said. "Ania's frightened. She can't manage without me."

"Yes. Oh, poor Ania! But . . . " She gazed up at me, her eyes filling with tears.

A car horn honked below.

"Here!" Twisting a little ring from her finger, she slipped it onto mine. It bore the double eagle of the Romanovs, and her initial, A. Then she held out her arms. "I'm not a grand duchess now, only an ex-, so I can hug whomever I like," she sobbed.

I tore myself away and ran from the room.

Ania was limping to the front door on her crutch, a footman supporting her other arm.

"Here I am, Ania," I cried, pushing him aside.

"Dunia!" she murmured, and I felt her arm tighten around my shoulder.

The big black car was surrounded by soldiers. I helped Ania in and handed her the crutch. As I started to climb in after her, a soldier shoved me back with the butt of his rifle. I stumbled, and landed on my hands and knees on the gravel.

The soldier gestured with his bayonet. "Get back inside the palace," he sneered. "She won't be needing a servant where she's going!" He slammed the door, and gravel sprayed under the wheels of the car as it sped off.

The last I saw of Ania was the pale moon of her face looking back at me through the rear window.

The days passed somehow, and spring came at last. Grass grew up through the stones of the courtyard, and the branches of unpruned trees hid the lower windows of the palace. It was as if a spell had been cast on us, and time stood still. The great events of the revolution seemed as distant as echoes.

Little by little our guards' hearts seemed to thaw toward us. The commander of the palace troops, Colonel Kobilynsky, was a kindly man, though he carried out his duties strictly. The soldiers of the 1st and 4th regiments became more and more friendly. Now the Tsar was allowed to walk as far as the little lake, and as the weather grew warmer his children joined him.

But Anastasia still had to stay in bed, so I kept her company.

"Come along now, Dunia," ordered Alexei one bright day. "We're rowing to the island."

"I'll come another time," I said, "when Anastasia can come too."

He frowned. "You're supposed to be *my* protégé, you know," he said, going to the door. Then he added, "But I suppose it's all right, as Nastasia's still sick."

I did go out another day, when the violets bloomed like a purple haze under the trees of the park. I picked her a huge bunch.

"Oh — violets!" She buried her little spotted face in them. Then, with a sly glance, "You love *me* the very best of all, don't you?" she demanded.

"Always," I told her.

"I thought so," she said, snuggling down among her pillows.

One day in late May, the Tsar said, "It seems we are going to be here for a long time yet. We should think about fuel for next winter, and fresh vegetables. Perhaps they'll allow us to plant a kitchen garden and cut down dead trees in the park."

"You'll do just about anything to get exercise, Papa," teased Anastasia. For now that the Tsar could not go for long walks or rides, he seemed as restless as a caged beast.

The soldiers thought it was a good joke to see the Tsar planting cabbages and sawing wood. They would gather around and give advice. One, pushing his cap back on his head said, "He knows how to work! If they gave him a *lopin* of land to farm he'd soon own all of Russia again!"

Sometimes Alexandra Feodorovna would sit outside in her wheelchair. Then the banter would stop, and the soldiers would stare at her as if she were a monster from a fairy tale. When she tried to chat with them about their families, they would scratch their heads and grow tongue-tied. "Nikolai Alexandrovich isn't much like a tsar," I heard one of them say to another. "But Alexandra Feodorovna — she's a real tsarina!"

I took pictures of it all: the soldiers staring at the Tsarina, the Tsar digging, Anastasia and Marie towing a water barrel . . .

Crowds often gathered along the park fence while we worked, jeering and pointing.

"Let's give them something to stare at," said Anastasia, grinning. She went over and whispered to her sisters, who nodded and laughed. She picked up her camera from the grass and handed it to me. "Take our picture, Dunia," she ordered. "Wait until I give the signal."

They stood in a row. "One . . . Two . . . Three!" chanted Anastasia. Just before the shutter clicked, they all whipped off the kerchiefs they were wearing. They were as bald as eggs!

I gasped and dropped the camera.

They all doubled over, laughing.

"You should see your face, Dunia!" said Olga, re-tying her kerchief.

"Mama had our hair cut off just before we came outside," explained Anastasia.

"It was coming out in clumps," Tatiana added, picking up her shovel. "From the measles, you know."

"It was disgusting!" Anastasia wrinkled her nose. "Much better to get rid of it all at once — only I'd just got old enough to wear mine up at last."

I crossed myself. Their bald heads all in a row had reminded me of dead bodies.

July was hot and sunny, and we ate the first lettuces from the kitchen garden. Then Kerensky arrived again, looking worried.

"*Now* what? Every time that man comes here, there's trouble," said Anastasia, looking up from a jig-saw puzzle. We pricked up our ears. There were few secrets in the palace now, for all the doors stood wide open with sentries posted outside.

"What's a Bolshevik?" I asked Olga. For I could hear Kerensky saying the word over and over.

She frowned. "An extreme revolutionary. Different from Kerensky's party."

"It seems we may have to leave after all," the Tsar told us, after Kerensky had gone away.

"We can't go now!" protested Anastasia. "My carrots aren't ready to be pulled!"

"Hush, Nastasia! What did he say, Nicky?" asked the Tsarina.

"The Bolsheviks are trying to take over the government. Kerensky wants to send us farther away from Petrograd. He said, 'The Bolsheviks are after me, and next they'll be after you!'"

The Tsarina sighed. "I'd just got used to Kerensky. Now it's Bolsheviks!"

"But where will they send us?" asked Alexei. "Can we go to Livadia?"

"Oh, could we?" cried Anastasia.

The Tsar shook his head. "Kerensky says it will be a town in the east." He looked down at the Tsarina. "We'll be there for the winter at least, my dear. Make sure there is plenty of warm clothing for all of us."

A few days later, the Tsar received another message from Kerensky. August 13 would be the day we left. Now the whole palace was turned upside down, as everyone tried to decide what to take and what had to be left behind. The remaining servants scurried from one room to another, packing clothing and carpets, pictures, lamps and keepsakes and then unpacking them again when people changed their minds.

They told us to be ready at ten-thirty that night. Our journey was so secret that the cars wouldn't come to pick us up until the very last minute. Mountains of luggage were piled in the round room at the front of the palace, and we all sat waiting. Ten-thirty came and went, and the cars didn't come. After an hour, they told us to put on our coats. But still the cars didn't appear.

"What's causing the delay?" the Tsar demanded of Colonel Kobilynsky.

The colonel shrugged. "I don't know, sir. Perhaps the railway workers wouldn't allow the train to leave Petrograd," he said.

"I'm hungry," protested Alexei, who was prowling around restlessly.

So we had tea, and then we waited some more. At last, just as the sky was beginning to grow light, a column of cars and trucks pulled up before the palace. The family was bundled into two cars, and I squeezed into another with the ladies-in-waiting. A cavalry escort surrounded us and we set out for the station. I stared back at the Alexander Palace, its windows reflecting the pale light of morning. It grew smaller and smaller behind us, as if seen through the wrong end of the Tsar's telescope. Then we turned a corner, and it vanished behind the trees.

19

Tobolsk

August – October, 1917

The train pulled out of Tsarskoe Selo at dawn.

"But where are we going, Papa?" asked Anastasia.

"To Tobolsk," said the Tsar. "In Siberia."

Siberia! It was as if Grigory had reached from his grave to put me back where he found me!

By afternoon, Petrograd lay far behind us, and the train was rolling through hot, dusty countryside. I sat listening to the clacking of the wheels, remembering my journey with Grigory. For we were going to Tiumen. From there we would take a steamer down the river to Tobolsk.

It became hotter and hotter. "Oof!" exclaimed Anastasia, straining to throw open the window.

"Close that!" ordered a guard. "We're passing a station." He made us pull the blinds down too, despite the heat, but peeping out, I glimpsed a platform lined with soldiers. At last, just after six in the evening, the train stopped.

"Where are we? Where are we?" everyone asked, peering out. There was no station in sight.

"You can get out and walk for an hour," the guards told us. So we all tumbled over each other to get off, and into the fresh air. Alexei took his dog, Joy, and Anastasia carried her little spaniel. The Tsar stepped out briskly and the rest of us trailed after him, the dogs running circles around us.

The journey seemed endless. Each day passed like the first. When the train reached the mountains, the air grew fresher. Finally we came out on the steppe.

"This is truly the soul of Russia," sighed the Tsarina, gazing out at the great meadowland stretching away to the horizon. "I feel closer to Grigory here."

Late in the evening of the fourth day, the train moved through Tiumen, and stopped by the river, where a steamboat was tied up at a jetty. We boarded it at once. With much banging and crashing and swearing, the luggage was loaded. At dawn the steamboat slipped out into the current. By the middle of the next day, we were far downriver. After lunch we all went on deck to watch the shore slide past.

"Look at that big village," said Anastasia, pointing. "I wonder what its name is."

My heart was heavy. I had known that we would have to pass it. "It's Pokrovskoe," I said.

"Mama, we're passing Father Grigory's village!" she called.

The Tsarina rushed to the rail. "Can it really be?" she gasped. "Nicky, give me your telescope!" She scanned the shore eagerly. "Which house is his, Dunia?" she demanded.

"That one," I said, pointing. I felt as if I was slipping backward through time.

Anastasia took the telescope. "Oh. I thought it would be bigger!"

"It *is* big," I said. "For Siberia."

The Tsarina leaned on the rail, her eyes clinging to the house as it slipped away upstream. "Grigory once told me we would all see his house in Siberia," she murmured to the Tsar. "I said it was too far for us to travel. But, you see, he was right — he was always right!"

At last we saw white-walled churches with onion domes clustered high on a hill, their gold crosses glittering against the sky. A town of log isbas sprawled along the riverbank below.

"Tobolsk," said Colonel Kobilynsky, squaring his shoulders.

The moment the steamboat tied up, Anastasia and Alexei demanded to go ashore. The Tsar shook his head. "Colonel Kobilynsky must inspect the house we are to live in," he said.

The colonel took a small detachment of guards, and walked up to the town. An hour later, he returned, shaking his head. "The house is empty and filthy. Nothing is ready for you," he said.

And so, while the colonel rushed about hiring workmen and buying furniture, we stayed aboard the boat. It wasn't until a week later that we saw our new home.

As we trudged up the hill, curious townspeople stared from behind the lines of soldiers. Many crossed themselves as the Tsar passed, and some fell to their knees.

The Governor's House was a large white stone building. The family were to live on the second floor, with the guards below them. Anastasia and Alexei bounded up the stairs, and I started to follow, but one of the guards lowered his rifle in front of me.

"Family and servants only in this house," he growled. "Ladies-in-waiting across the street."

I rolled my eyes. "Look at me, brother," I said. "Do I look like a lady-in-waiting?"

His eyes narrowed. "You're a servant?" he asked. "What kind?"

"I'm a maid," I said, thinking fast. "And I help in the kitchen too."

"Is that right, Colonel?" the man demanded of Kobilynsky, who had come up behind us.

I looked pleadingly at the colonel.

"Why . . . yes," he replied. "Dunia serves the grand duchesses."

"Carry their luggage, then," said the guard. Picking up a large suitcase, he dropped it into my arms, nearly flattening me. Then he guffawed as I wrestled it upstairs.

OTMA would share a corner room, and Alexei had one to himself. The Tsar and Tsarina had a bedroom, and each had another room for a study. The dining room was downstairs.

"It's not so bad," said Alexei.

"It's not so good," retorted Anastasia. "Did you see the bathroom?"

"*I* think it's cozy," said Marie. She sighed. "You know, I could almost be happy in Tobolsk — if we were free."

That first day the kind-hearted colonel let the family explore the house and garden and cross the street to visit the ladies- and gentlemen-in-waiting in their house. But the soldiers of the 2nd regiment protested. After that they told us that the family could only leave the house once a week, to go to church.

On Sunday, we walked out in a little procession, the Tsar and the Tsarina in the lead and the rest of us straggling after then. The guards hemmed us in on both sides, and closed in right behind us. After we had gone just a little way, Anastasia turned around and baahed at the soldiers. They looked puzzled, and the commissar in charge scowled at her.

"Well, you herd us like a flock of sheep," she huffed, stalking on ahead.

The soldiers also built a tall plank fence on one side of the house, between it and the street. The family had to take all their exercise there, where no one could see them. The Tsar asked for logs to be brought, and everyone took turns sawing wood for the winter.

"If we could only go for a real walk!" said Anastasia, gazing out the window at the golden autumn hills. "I'm getting as fat as a pig just pacing in the yard!" For she was now as stout as Marie had once been, and she still hadn't grown much.

As for me, I got plenty of exercise running up and down stairs. When I wasn't dusting and tidying, I helped in the kitchen, carrying trays and tureens. I often smuggled treats up to the family, for sugar and cakes, butter and eggs poured in from kindly townspeople. When my work was done, I was free to go about in the town, which I saw pretty thoroughly in an hour. There was a Big Mud Street and a Little Mud Street, and people pattered around on wooden sidewalks.

On one of my afternoons out, I saw a man laden with suitcases and bundles toiling uphill from the steamboat landing. "Gibbsy!" I cried, running to help him. "Where have you been?"

"I was stranded in Petrograd when the palace was closed," he explained, mopping his brow. "It's taken me all this time to get here!"

Soon friends began to send letters for the family to servants who lived in the town. I smuggled them in and out, for the soldiers never bothered to search me as they did the others. One day I recognized Ania's handwriting on a letter, and I hung about while the Tsarina read it. A soldier of the 2nd regiment scowled at me suspiciously, so I whipped a duster out of my apron pocket and set to work on the legs of her table. "Please, Alexandra Feodorovna, how is Ania?" I whispered.

"She has suffered terribly," said the Tsarina. "They kept her in prison for months, poor soul, but couldn't prove a thing against her. So at last they let her go."

"God be praised!" I said. For the thought of poor

foolish Ania in prison had been hard to bear.

"But she sends great news," the Tsarina went on, with a quick glance to make sure the guard wasn't listening. "A man is coming to help us escape."

"Escape?" I jerked my head up, cracking it on the table.

Anastasia pricked up her ears. She came over and sat down beside her mother.

"Shhh!" warned the Tsarina. "Yes. I think he has arrived in Tobolsk. Someone has handed my maid a package from Ania with a little money and warm clothing. Dunia must help us now."

"But what do you want her to do?" asked Anastasia.

"Go to this man — Soloviev is his name — and find out if he is the one Ania spoke of in her letter. If he is, tell him to go ahead with the Brotherhood of St. John."

"But how can I tell if he is the man?" I asked.

"Ask him to describe Marochka Rasputina," replied the Tsarina. "Soloviev is her husband."

Marochka had a husband! "But where do I find this Soloviev?"

"He's at nine Tobol Ulitsky. Give him this," she added, slipping a religious medal into my hand.

That same afternoon, I found my way to Tobol Ulitsky. Number 9 was a one-storey log isba like all the others. I tapped on the door, which opened a crack.

"Who is it?" a man's voice demanded.

"I have something for the man who knows Ania," I said.

"Give it to me." The door opened wider, and a hand appeared. I dropped the medal into it. "St. John of Tobolsk!" the voice said. Then the door was flung open.

He was a tall, fair man with a moustache. "Your name is Soloviev?" I asked.

"Inside," he said. He closed the door behind me. "Now, what does the Tsarina say?"

"Why, nothing at all." I replied. "Unless you can tell me what Maria Grigorievna Rasputina looks like. And what her nickname is."

He gave me a toothy smile. "That's easy! My dear wife has bright pink cheeks, curls the colour of honey, and big grey eyes. Her friends call her Marochka. Do you know her, then?"

I nodded. "I saw her at her father's apartment."

His face became solemn. "Grigory Efimovich, our martyred saint," he murmured, crossing himself. "You are blessed to have known him. But what did the Tsarina say?"

"She wants you to go ahead with the Brotherhood of St. John."

"Good, good," he said. "I will see to it all! I have three hundred loyal officers in Tiumen, ready to act at a moment's notice. But we must have arms and supplies. Ania and our other friends in Petrograd must send money. Then we will whisk the family away!"

"Soldiers guard them closely," I pointed out.

"I know, I know! Still, we will rescue them. Then we can take them on sledges to Murmansk. Or even better, by train to Vladivostock and then to Japan . . . "

Sledges all the way to Murmansk in winter? A train to Vladivostock? Was he crazy?

"Now run along and tell the Tsarina what I have said," ordered Soloviev. "I must return to Tiumen, where I can keep an eye on the trains and the telegraph office. But I will return soon. How can I reach you?"

"My name is Dunia Ivanovna. Leave messages for me with the cook, Kharitonov," I told him.

"Fine," said Soloviev, grinning. "To the Brotherhood of St. John!" he added, all but pushing me out the door.

Alexandra Feodorovna was alone, as all the others were outside taking exercise in the fenced yard. Through the windows I could see OTMA in their red and blue angora tams and grey capes. Olga and Tatiana were tramping back and forth with the Tsar, while Anastasia and Marie chatted with the guards.

"Was he the man? What did he say?" demanded the Tsarina.

"He is Soloviev," I told her. "I gave him the medal. He said he has three hundred loyal officers waiting in Tiumen, but they need more money from your friends in Petrograd."

"They will get it! We won't be forgotten," said Alexandra Feodorovna, smiling.

"He says he might take you to Murmansk, or maybe to Vladivostock," I said doubtfully.

"I'm sure he knows what he's doing!" The Tsarina sank back among her cushions. "Oh, it is hard to wait," she said. "But at least we can wait in hope. Thank you, Dunia," she added, her eyes suddenly filling with tears. "I never forget, you know, that you are the priceless gift of our beloved Grigory."

I never did, either. Would I ever be free of Grigory's shadow?

20

Ice

November, 1917 – April, 1918

The Tsarina waited eagerly, but we heard no more from Soloviev. Week after week passed. The weather stayed fine, but although the days were golden, the news was not. The rough local newspaper began to quote telegrams about another Bolshevik revolt in Petrograd.

"How can anyone trust blackguards like the Bolsheviks?" the Tsar murmured. "Surely Kerensky's government will quash this revolt as it did the last."

But then a huge package of Petrograd newspapers arrived, and we learned that Kerensky's government had been overturned by the Bolsheviks, and he had fled Petrograd.

The Tsar read the papers in silence. But Zhilik, the French tutor, had more to say. I had got to know Zhilik much better since we left Tsarskoe Selo. He knew a lot about politics, and I sometimes asked him to explain things to me.

"Are the Bolsheviks bad?" I asked him one day.

"Bad for the Tsar, yes," he said, frowning. "Kerensky was a moderate, and did not want violence. The Bolsheviks will do anything to create the new Russia they dream of. The Tsar is a political hostage. God knows what they will decide to do with him."

Despite the grim news, the Tsarina was serene. I knew she had put her faith in Soloviev and his three hundred officers.

By December, Tobolsk was buried in snow. A fire burned all day in the sitting room, but it couldn't defeat the Siberian cold. We shivered when we woke up, we shivered all day and we shivered in bed.

"We lie under the covers listening to each other's teeth chattering," joked Anastasia. "It's even worse than Mashka's snoring."

Everyone began to make preparations for Christmas. The Tsarina and OTMA made little gifts for everybody, and Alexei wrapped up items from his collection of objects. "You see, my things *are* useful," he said, when Zhilik teased him.

On Christmas Eve, the family decorated a small tree, and took it down to the guards on duty, along with some good things to eat. The soldiers of the friendly 4th regiment talked wistfully of their own families far away.

In January, the outdoor temperature dropped to minus sixty-eight. "I'm bored with sawing wood and tramping to and fro in the yard," complained Anastasia. "Why don't we make a snow mountain as we used to do at Tsarskoe?"

"Would the guards let us?" I asked.

She grinned. "I'll get Mashka to ask. She's their favourite — they're sure to say yes to her!"

It took ten days to build the mountain, and everybody helped. The soldiers of the 4th pushed wheelbarrows of snow while OTMA, Alexei and I ran back and forth with buckets and shovels. Then the Tsar and Zhilik iced the slope with buckets of water. It was so cold that the water sometimes froze solid before they reached the hill.

The Tsar had knocked some sleds together out of odd bits of wood. We hurled ourselves down the slope, screaming with laughter when we piled up at the bottom. Anastasia ambushed Alexei with a snowball, and the rest of us joined in. We all ended up rolling in the snow.

Anastasia was still restless. "We need something to do in the evenings," she sighed. "They're so long and dark. And we can't read or sew *all* the time."

"We used to act scenes from plays," said Marie. "You were good, Nastasia."

"Now, why didn't *I* think of that?" she cried. She was on her feet in an instant, pacing back and forth. "Gibbsy and Zhilik have books of plays, so that part's all set. Everybody must act or help with the costumes or do *something*. We'll be a real theatre company."

She arranged it all, and coaxed the others to take part. The actors would learn and rehearse their lines after tea, and the performances would be on Sunday evenings after dinner.

"Pick short plays," said Alexei. "I go to bed at nine, and I don't want to miss anything!"

Anastasia's favourite play was called *Packing Up*. Marie played the wife, and Anastasia, in Gibbsy's old dressing gown, played the husband. From behind the bedspread curtain, we could hear a buzz of conversation. Family, ladies- and gentlemen-in-waiting, servants and the commandant were all crowded into the dining room.

At Anastasia's signal, I pulled a rope, and the curtain slid aside. The play went off beautifully. Marie made a perfect wife, and Anastasia, a swaggering husband. At the end, turning her back to the audience, she flung the dressing gown open with a flourish and cried, "I've packed my trousers. I can't go!" Just then, a stray draft caught the tail of the robe and flipped it halfway up her back. And there was her big bottom in a pair of the Tsar's long underwear!

The audience roared — the Tsarina nearly fell out of her chair laughing. Wild applause followed, with loud calls for another performance.

Anastasia took her bow looking puzzled. "I'm glad they liked my acting," she said. "But the last line isn't *that* funny!"

I never told her.

At long last there came a message from Soloviev, asking me to meet him. He appeared in the doorway of the isba wearing a rich fur overcoat.

"Listen," he said, as he closed the door behind me. "The Tsarina isn't playing fair with me. Those fine friends of hers haven't sent any more money. How can I pay my officers?"

"But she *did* write asking for money. I smuggled the letters out myself!"

"Well, it hasn't come," he said. "And here's another thing. Some fools of officers from Tiumen don't believe I speak for the Tsarina. I've brought them to Tobolsk to prove it. She must step out on the balcony and give this sign." He made a gesture with his right hand.

"The Tsarina can't go outside — her heart is too weak to stand the cold!" I protested.

Soloviev shrugged. "One of the grand duchesses, then." he said. "The little one — Anastasia. She must come out on the balcony at three o'clock sharp, and give the signal. Or it's goodbye to the Brotherhood of St. John." He handed over a few small packages and showed me the door.

"But he *must* have received money," said the Tsarina. "Ania sent some, and other friends, too."

I remembered Soloviev's fur coat, and my heart sank. What if he was keeping the money for himself?

Anastasia eagerly practised the secret signal. "This is better than a play!" she exclaimed. At the appointed hour she opened the French windows and stepped out on the balcony. She gave the signal once, then again, then twice more.

"Get back in here!" I hissed, dragging her by the arm. "What if one of the guards saw you?"

"There were some men in the street," she reported. "A big fellow in a fur coat nodded to me."

"What was all that about?" Zhilik asked later. So I told him. "Three hundred loyal officers in Tiumen?" he said, frowning. "I doubt it. I fear this Soloviev is a rogue. Where are the real friends of the Tsar and Tsarina? Why don't they act? Soon it may be too late!"

That very week the Bolshevik government sent new troops to replace our guards.

"Mashka's heartbroken," Anastasia confided to me. "Most of the men of our regiments are in love with her."

Many soldiers slipped in secretly to say goodbye. When they marched away, the Tsar climbed to the top of the snow mountain to see them off. Braving the cold, the Tsarina insisted on going with him.

The new troops reacted quickly. The next morning they began destroying the mountain with pick-axes.

"It's too dangerous to leave it," an officer told us, grinning. "Someone might shoot one of you from the street when you're standing on top of it."

"What a mean thing to do!" Alexei cried, clutching the sled the Tsar had made for him.

It was as if the new guards had orders to make us as miserable as possible. Filthy words and drawings appeared on the fence, and even on the seats of the swing that OTMA used in warm weather. The upstairs toilet blocked up, and to use the one downstairs the girls had to pass the guards, who stared rudely and said dirty words to them.

The newspapers said the Bolsheviks had signed a

peace treaty with Germany. The Tsar's face turned grey when he read about it. "They've abandoned our allies, and given away a third of our country to the Germans!" he said bitterly, "My abdication was for nothing, then!" At last he crossed himself. "All my life I tried to do my best for Russia," he said. "I bow to God's will."

Not long afterwards, a line of *troikas* dashed past the house, sleigh bells tinkling gaily on the horses' harness. "It must be our rescuers at last," breathed the Tsarina, staring down at them eagerly. "I can feel it! Just look at their good Russian faces!"

Zhilik went down to the street, but returned shaking his head. "They are commissars from Omsk," he said. "Come to educate the people about Bolshevism."

The Tsarina's face fell. "But still," she said, "there may be loyal officers among them!"

It seemed as if that bleak winter would never end. Carnival time came, and we all listened wistfully to the sounds of merry-making in the streets. Next came Lent, and the Tsarina would allow no more plays to be put on.

"I know Mama is right," sighed Anastasia. "But it was the only fun we had left."

OTMA took turns sitting in the window watching people in the street. When passers-by noticed them and bowed, the guards would chase them away. Day after weary day, Marie pined for her friendly soldiers. Olga snapped at the others, and tried to lose herself in books. Tatiana said nothing to anyone, and became razor thin, as if she were wearing away from inside.

Anastasia played more and more pranks. The little shvipsik put salt in the sugar bowls, and watched our faces with glee when we put it on our porridge. She tied knots in her sisters' sheets so they couldn't get into their beds, and smuggled in a stone from the yard, which she slipped, icy-cold, into the bottom of Alexei's. She soaped the soles of my shoes, so that I skidded halfway across the dining room, dropped the soup tureen, and sat down in a puddle of borscht. She particularly loved to torment poor Gibbsy, talking non-stop through every lesson until he lost his temper and told her to shut up. Delighted, she adopted "Shut up!" as her motto, and wrote it on all her lesson books. She even made a song of it and sang it loudly at the piano.

"How *can* you go on this way?" I groaned. For though we all laughed at her nonsense, I sometimes wanted to shake her.

She shot me a glance from under her level brows. "I thought you would understand," she said. "Don't you see that I *have* to? They expect it of me."

I squeezed her hand. I should have guessed what she was about.

I often heard Alexei shouting at the tutors. He took to riding his sled down the inside stairs. It made a hideous noise, and there was a terrific crash each time he hit the bottom. The Tsarina begged him not to do it, but he ignored her. After watching her turn pale and cross herself, I ran down the stairs after him

"*Must* you do this, Alexei Nikolaevich?" I demanded. "You're frightening your mother!"

"Oh, she's always frightened," he said, shrugging. He started up the stairs again with the sled.

I yanked on the tail of his tunic. "But you may get hurt, and have that awful pain again . . . "

He turned on me, his eyes wild with rage. "Let go of me!" he snarled.

I let go.

"It doesn't matter," he sighed, the fire going out of his eyes. "Nothing matters anymore!" Then he burst into tears and ran upstairs.

That night, I found a beautifully coiled piece of copper wire on my pillow. It was one of his favourite things. But the next day the sliding began again, and the day after, he slipped and hurt himself, and began to bleed.

It was Spala all over again. But this time there was no Grigory to help. Alexei's cries pierced our ears for days.

Still more troops arrived in April, and last of all came a commissar called Yakovlev. Tall and muscular, with jet black hair, he spoke politely to the Tsar and Tsarina, and insisted on visiting Alexei. The air felt electric. Something was going to happen.

Anastasia burned her letters and her diary. "If that new commissar thinks he's going to read *my* private papers, he's going to be disappointed," she vowed.

"Oh, where are Soloviev and his officers?" lamented the Tsarina. "Why doesn't the Brotherhood of St. John *do* something?"

The next day Yakovlev revealed his mission: he was supposed to take the family to Moscow. Because Alexei was ill, he would take the Tsar alone. The rest of the family could follow later.

"I refuse to leave my family," said the Tsar.

"I beg you not to refuse," Yakovlev said quietly. "For then I shall either have to take you by force, or resign. And the next commissar will be harsher than I. You must leave tomorrow."

The Tsarina was in agony. "They will take him to Moscow and try to make him sign that hideous peace treaty," she cried. "And they will threaten us to make him do it! I can't let him go alone — but how can I leave Alexei?"

Back and forth she paced, and even Tatiana was unable to calm her.

"The Tsarevich is a bit better," said Zhilik. "If you go, we will all take the greatest care of him."

"That's right, Mama," said Tatiana. "And Zhilik and Gibbsy will watch over us. We'll be fine, truly we will."

The Tsarina stopped pacing. "Yes. No matter what they do to the Tsar or to me, I'm sure they'll never harm the children," she said to Zhilik. "Very well, then, I'll go with Nicky. I'll take Marie with me — she can stand a rough journey. Olga will see to Alexei, and Tatiana can look after the household."

"What about me, Mama?" cried Anastasia. "Can't I help too?"

"*You* will keep everyone cheered up," said the Tsarina, with the ghost of a smile.

The carriages that would take them to the train at Tiumen arrived at dawn, and they were nothing but wretched tarantasses!

The Tsar shook the hands of all his men, and the Tsarina kissed all the women. Then they clambered into the carts, the Tsar riding with Yakovlev, and the Tsarina with Marie. A cavalry escort surrounded the carts. Whips cracked, wheels creaked, and they disappeared into the morning mist.

21

Ekaterinburg

May – June, 1918

"Mama writes that we must dispose of the medicines," said Tatiana, looking up from her letter.

"But where?" asked Olga, frowning.

"In places the guards won't look," said Tatiana. "Inside hats, cushions . . . "

"Why not in our corsets and underwear?" asked Anastasia, grinning.

"Really, Nastasia!" said Tatiana, raising her eyebrows.

"No, she's right," said Olga. "Why not?"

"What are you talking about?" I demanded. "*What* medicines?"

Olga and Tatiana exchanged a quick glance, but Anastasia said, "Oh, don't be stupid. Of course we can tell Dunia!" Then, lowering her voice, she whispered, "Medicines is a code word for jewels."

Tatiana nodded. "We brought jewels with us to Tobolsk," she said. "We'll have to sell them to get money to live on, you see. So we have to take them with us when we go to Ekaterinburg."

For the Tsar and Tsarina and Marie had not been taken to Moscow after all. Their train from Tiumen had been stopped along the way, and now, in May, they were prisoners in Ekaterinburg, a small city in the Ural Mountains. We were eager to join them as soon as Alexei could travel, for without the others we were like scattered puzzle pieces, too few to make a picture ourselves.

We set to work to hide the "medicines." We covered rubies with cloth to make buttons, and stitched diamonds and emeralds into cushions and hatbands. Ropes of pearls were turned into belts that the girls could wear under their dresses.

Anastasia gleefully stitched gems into the ribs of her corsets and the hems of her petticoats. "I'm as heavy as an elephant!" she exclaimed, stomping about.

We finished not a moment too soon, for the first day Alexei was well enough to sit in a wheelchair, the commissar in charge of us said we must leave for Ekaterinburg. We would travel to Tiumen on the same boat that had brought us to Tobolsk eight months before.

We spent two days on the river, and I took snapshot after snapshot of my dear ones. And then there was no more film in the camera.

At Tiumen, soldiers surrounded us as we walked to a waiting train. Nagorny had to carry Alexei, who still couldn't walk. "Only family in this carriage," a commissar barked at me as I tried to climb into the train after Anastasia. I saw her face pressed white against the window as the rest of us were led away.

I was put into a luggage car with Zhilik and Gibbsy and the servants. Guards slammed the doors, and with a jolt the train began to move forward. All through the long day we rocked and swayed on hard benches. At last, late in the evening, the train came to a stop.

"They've pulled past the station," said Zhilik, peering out the window.

Hour after hour we sat. At dawn we heard carriages approaching. Rubbing at the mist on the window, I stared out. Rain was pouring down. Through it I saw Nagorny carrying Alexei toward a line of droshkies. Behind him Olga and Anastasia struggled through the mud with heavy suitcases. Last of all came Tatiana, dragging another suitcase, with Anastasia's little spaniel, Jimmy, under her arm. They climbed in, and the droshkies drove off.

"Let us out!" Zhilik demanded. "We must go with them."

The guards just laughed. Soon more droshkies arrived. Now the ladies- and gentlemen-in-waiting were marched from another railway carriage and driven away.

Zhilik approached one of our guards. "Where are they taking those people?" he asked.

The man grinned. "Why, to prison. And then . . . " And he drew his forefinger across his throat.

An hour passed, and then it was our turn. The doors opened, and a guard shouted, "Servants next! The rest of you stay where you are."

"God be with you, Dunia," I heard Zhilik say as I stumbled toward the door.

Five of us plodded through the mud toward the droshkies, carrying our small bundles.

Our droshky drove through street after dingy street. At last it turned up a hill and stopped in front of a big stone house behind a tall fence of wooden planks.

"Is this the prison?" I asked a guard.

He shook his head. "It's the Ipatiev house," he replied. "But it has a new name now. They call it The House of Special Purpose."

They marched us upstairs to the second floor. There was a room with three guards at the top. Ugly blue-black revolvers lay on the table before them.

"They're in there. Go ahead and lick their boots!" sneered one of the guards, jerking his thumb toward the next room.

We walked through an empty chamber, through an archway . . . And there they were, all my dear ones together again. The puzzle was complete once more.

"Dunia, you slowpoke! What took you so long?" demanded Anastasia, hugging me.

"Where's Zhilik? I want Zhilik!" clamoured Alexei.

"And the others — where are they?" asked the Tsarina.

"Zhilik and Gibbsy are still on the train," I faltered. "The others were taken to prison."

"Oh, no!" gasped Marie. The Tsarina turned pale, and her hand crept over her heart

"Surely they will send them back to us soon, Mama," Tatiana said quickly. "Meanwhile, we must think where twelve people can sleep in five rooms!"

The cook and the footman had to sleep in a hall. As for me, I slept on the floor of the maid's room. She seemed glad to have someone to talk to.

"I'm so afraid of what these Bolsheviks are going to do to us, Dunia," she whispered, "It's terrible here — much worse than Tobolsk!"

I soon saw that for myself. Avdeyev, the commander of the guards, was a bully and a drunkard. He made us all eat from a common dish, often shoving the Tsar aside to snatch pieces of food with his fingers. His men wandered in and out of our rooms at will, staring at us with hostile eyes and saying rude things. Even worse, we had to pass the guards on duty every time we wanted to use the toilet.

"Here come Fatty and Skinny again," a guard said as Anastasia and I went by one morning.

"We've decorated the walls of the toilet for you!" the other added, grinning.

They had scrawled filthy drawings of the Tsarina and Grigory on the walls. Pulling out her handkerchief, Anastasia tried to scrub them away, but they wouldn't come off. Furious, she pounded on the wall with both fists. "Why do they have to be so hateful, *why?*" she muttered.

Playthings for the cat, but tears for the mouse, I

thought.

"I try to be resigned, like Mama," Anastasia went on, "but I keep wanting to knock their heads together!"

"They are dedicated Bolsheviks," Dr. Botkin explained, when we told him what the guards had done. "They have been taught to hate the Tsar and the Tsarina bitterly." He sighed. "They are factory workers, not professional soldiers, and have lived hard lives from the time they were children. No one has ever pitied them, and so they pity no one. We must bear it as best we can."

That evening the guards started bawling filthy songs. Anastasia jumped to her feet, her cheeks flaming. At the top of her voice she began to sing "The Cherubim Song," a hymn the Tsarina dearly loved. Olga rose to her feet and joined in. Tatiana and Marie followed. Arms around each others' waists, they sang to their mother, who sat beating time. When the hymn was finished, they sang another. There was silence from the guardroom.

"That's right, girlies," said the Tsarina, nodding. "Sing them down. *Live* them down."

Not all the guards tormented us. There was one, younger than the rest, who never did. He was a tall fellow, with a mop of shaggy brown hair that kept escaping from under his cap. He was stiffly correct with us, though when he looked at the Tsar, his eyes were hot and hating.

One day we were coming back from exercise in the garden. I was struggling to keep hold of Joy's leash,

222

and I had Jimmy the spaniel under my arm. Joy jerked his leash out of my hand and bounded ahead of me up to the guards' room. I raced after him, clutching Jimmy.

At the top of the stairs, I froze. Joy was happily sniffing the muddy boots of one of the guards, who had drawn his revolver from its holster and was pointing it at him.

"Don't!" I cried. "Please don't!"

The guard looked up. "Will you give me a kiss if I don't, Skinny?" he smirked.

"Let her alone, Kiriyenko." The other guard, the brown-haired one, picked up the end of Joy's leash and handed it to me. "Keep better hold of him," he said gruffly, and turned away before I could thank him.

"That young guard follows you with his eyes, Dunia," Maric told me later.

"Nonsense, Marie Nikolaevna!" I said.

"Mashka's always looking for romance — and finding it," said Anastasia, grinning. "But she's right. That boy does watch you. Haven't you noticed?"

I hadn't, but after that I couldn't help it. Marie was right. But his expression was puzzled rather than admiring. And he always scowled when he caught me looking at him.

In June the weather became hot and then hotter. Our windows were whitewashed and tightly sealed, so the rooms became terribly stuffy. Our only relief was the half hour of exercise we were allowed morning and afternoon in the dusty little garden.

"Surely we could have at least one window open," said the Tsar. "I'm going to ask."

At first the answer was no. But then a committee of several guards arrived to look the situation over. They scratched their heads and went away. A commissar came from the town, and then another committee.

"If this is the way Bolsheviks make decisions, I don't see how they manage to run the country," sighed the Tsar.

At last a guard told us that the plank fence around the house would be made taller, and then we would be allowed to open one window. For days they hammered and banged away at the fence, and then one stifling afternoon they came and opened the window. There had been a brief shower, and a rain-washed breeze scented with lilacs flowed in to replace the stale air and kitchen smells we had breathed for so long.

"At last!" said Anastasia. Perching on the window sill, she poked her head out. Instantly, a shot was fired, and a bullet ploughed into the window frame beside her. She jumped back in.

"If you put your heads out the window or sit on the sill, the window will be closed again," the young guard told us, frowning.

Anastasia stuck her tongue out when he turned his back. "Spoilsport!" she muttered.

And still the young guard watched me. It became a little joke between the Tsar and Dr. Botkin. "I really think he'll get up the nerve to speak to her today," the Tsar said, with a sly glance in my direction. "Don't you agree?"

"Hmm." The doctor pursed his lips. "He's a very severe young man. I wouldn't bet on it — even if I had anything left to bet with."

I noticed that when we were out in the garden now my fellow-prisoners drifted away, leaving me on my own. They were trying to encourage him! It was very embarrassing.

And so I was sitting by myself when the guard at last came up to me.

"I'm Kolya Ilyich Kuriagin," he announced.

I shrugged. "I'm Dunia Ivanovna," I said. "But then you know that already."

"Why do you serve Nikolai the Blood-Drinker and the German woman?" he burst out.

"He is my Tsar and she is my Tsarina," I said.

"You are an enemy of the people, then," he accused.

"I *am* the people," I snapped, jumping to my feet. "I'm a peasant!"

His mouth dropped open. "You are?"

"Trust a Bolshevik not to know one when he sees one," I snorted, and walked away.

"Well? Well?" demanded Anastasia when I rejoined her. "What did he say? It looked as though you quarrelled."

"He's an idiot," I muttered, and wouldn't say more.

The next afternoon, he came up to me again. "No, wait," he said, when I started to walk away. "It's the duty of a revolutionary to think. I want to understand. You . . . You seem to be a decent girl . . . "

"Oh, *thank* you!" I tossed my head.

"What I mean is . . . You love these people. I can see that. Why?"

I sighed. It was an honest question and deserved an answer. "Because they are good people, and have been kind to me. And besides, you can't help who you love."

"That's true. You can't." He took off his cap, then put it on again. "But the Tsar is evil — "

I shook my head. "He's not! Can't you see that for yourself?"

He shifted his rifle on his shoulder. "But he wanted the war. He wanted to spill the blood of the Russian people!" he protested, frowning.

"The whole family cried when war was declared," I said simply.

"The Tsarina had Rasputin as her lover," he added. "And betrayed secrets to the Germans."

"That never happened," I said. "Not any of it!"

"You're lying," he snapped, and turning on his heel, he strode away.

For a day he turned away whenever he saw me, but the next, he handed me a cornflower from the garden. As he did, I noticed his hands were criss-crossed with ugly purple scars.

"You're not a liar," he muttered, blushing.

"No, I'm not," I said. Then I pointed to his hands and asked, "What are those scars?"

He shrugged. "I'm a metal-worker," he said. "I

have been since I was eight. Our gloves are small protection against hot sharp metal."

Eight! The thought of a little boy with cut and burned hands brought sudden tears to my eyes.

After that we talked for a little while each day he was on duty. I told him whatever he wanted to know as best I could. The other guards sniggered, but let us be. And little by little things began to change with them too. Though they still strolled through our rooms and stared at us, they made fewer cruel remarks.

"I almost dare to think they're becoming friendlier," said the Tsarina.

That didn't stop Avdeyev from getting drunk again and forgetting to order meat for us for two days. We had to survive on macaroni that the cook, Kharitonov, had brought from Tobolsk.

"I think I'm just a *little* thinner," said Anastasia afterward, inspecting herself in the mirror. "Don't you? And a bit taller?" For although she was seventeen now and wore her hair up she was still the malenkaya.

To help pass the long days, the girls decided to help Kharitonov in the kitchen. They made a big mess, but he bore it patiently. Little Lyonka Sednev, the kitchen boy, retreated awe-struck to a corner.

The first project OTMA tried was baking bread.

"I like this!" Anastasia announced, walloping her dough on the wooden table. "Kneading helps get my feelings out."

"Not too hard, Anastasia Nikolaevna," warned the

cook. "Or the bread will be like a stone."

"It's buns I'm making," she said. I noticed that when she set them to rise she had put an extra dab of dough on the top of one. "This one is special," she said, giving me a wink.

At dinner, Dr. Botkin broke open his bun, and there in the middle of it was his watch fob. "Why, I must have lost it," he said, patting his watch chain. "But how . . . ?" Then, "*Who* made these buns?" he growled, peering suspiciously over his glasses. "It must be . . . Anastasia Nikolaevna!"

Even then the little shvipsik made them smile.

22

Bars

June – July 15, 1918

One day in late June the Tsar found a mysterious note in the salon. "It tells us to be prepared for rescue," he said in a low voice, when he had gathered us all together.

"Nicky, it must be the Brotherhood of St. John at last!" breathed the Tsarina.

"It is signed only, 'An Officer'," replied the Tsar.

Soon other letters appeared, as if by magic. A rope ladder would be fastened to our window, they said. At a signal, we must barricade the doors with furniture, and flee.

"We cannot possibly escape without help," said the Tsar. "Alexei cannot walk. But we must be ready in case someone really does come to rescue us."

The night of June 27 was the appointed time. We only pretended to go to sleep, lying fully dressed under the covers, our hearts beating fast with excitement. But the hours ticked slowly by and nothing happened. At dawn we stared into each other's exhausted faces.

"Did something go wrong?" whispered the Tsarina. "Or . . . Were the letters only a trick, a cruel joke by the guards?"

The Tsar shook his head wearily. "I don't know," he murmured. "I simply don't know."

And so hope, which had sprung up like a bright blade of grass between stones, died again.

Our guards seemed strangely nervous now.

"What is it? What's wrong with all of you?" I asked Kolya when next I saw him.

He glanced both ways before he answered. "It's the White Army," he said in a low voice.

I knew the Bolshevik army was called the Red Army, but had never heard of a White Army. "Who are they?" I asked.

"They are fighting against the Bolsheviks, against the Revolution. They have defeated our Red Army at Tiumen, and they may be coming here next!"

"Whites fighting in Siberia!" mused the Tsar, when I told him. "I know there is civil war in the west. The White Army is trying to defeat the Bolsheviks in the Ukraine. But I didn't know there was a White Army here."

"It's good news, isn't it?" said Anastasia, her eyes lighting up. "The Whites will rescue us!"

"I hope so," said the Tsar. There was a faraway look in his eyes.

I was disappointed that he didn't seem happier at my news. Later I asked Dr. Botkin why the Tsar would be so unexcited by what I'd told him. "I thought he would be so pleased the Whites are winning!"

"He is . . . He is," murmured the doctor. "But you see, Dunia, if the Whites win, the Red Army — our guards and other soldiers — will have to pull out of Ekaterinburg. They'll never let the Whites capture the Tsar. They'll have to take him with them, or . . ." He shook his head.

Or *what?* A nameless fear began to grow inside me.

Two days later, a commissar named Yurovsky appeared with Avdeyev, who introduced him to the Tsar and Tsarina. A burly man with dark hair and a bushy beard, Yurovsky spoke politely, and seemed to make a good impression on everyone.

"He looks like a big black ox, but he has better manners than Avdeyev, anyway," whispered Anastasia, looking up from her photograph album.

"A pig has better manners than Avdeyev," I muttered.

The commissar stopped and looked down at Anastasia's album. She spoke up boldly. "Mr. Commissar, may we have our cameras back now? And some film so we can take pictures?"

"We'll see," he said, idly turning a page of the album. "Maybe *I'll* take your picture some day. I'm a photographer, too, you know."

I gazed up at him, and in that instant my fear sprang from its hiding place. For his eyes were as inhumanly cold as a camera lens. What I read in Yurovsky's eyes was death. I knew it as surely as a broken-winged bird sees death in the eyes of a snake.

231

A moment later, he had left the room. I began to tremble.

"You're all backwards, Dunia," joked Anastasia. "People shiver in January, not July!"

Kolya, I've got to talk to Kolya! was all I could think. The moment our exercise period began, I dragged him to one side. The other guards smirked and whistled.

"Who is that man Yurovsky?" I demanded.

Kolya's brown eyes were troubled. "He's the new commandant," he said. "We are being replaced. We are accused of being too lax, too kind to the prisoners — "

"Replaced! Are you going away? Have the Whites won?"

He shook his head. "Not yet. We will be posted next door in the Popov house. Yurovsky will bring in ten of his own men to guard the prisoners inside this house."

"You can't leave us to the mercy of that man!" I gasped, clutching his tunic. "He's a killer. I know it. I feel it, Kolya!"

"He's of the Cheka, the secret police. Even Avdeyev is afraid of him," he admitted. "But — "

"Look at these people. *Look!*" I cried, pointing to the other side of the yard. Alexei, still too weak to walk, was sunning himself in his mother's wheelchair. The Tsar was marching to and fro with his fast military stride. On either side of him, Anastasia and Marie jogged to keep up.

"Think what they have already lost," I went on,

more quietly. "Must they be punished more?"

"Even now, they still live better than any peasant," Kolya muttered.

"But so do plenty of other people. Must they all suffer too? These are good people, Kolya."

He turned away and scuffed the toe of his boot in the dust. "I do think differently now than I did before," he admitted. "The Tsar's government was wrong, but he and the Tsarina aren't evil. And the girls and the boy are innocent — "

"Then do something to help them!" I begged.

"What?" he cried. Then, quickly lowering his voice, "What *can* I do?"

I took a deep breath. "Go to the Whites," I said. "Tell them about Yurovsky. Tell them to send a rescue force quickly, oh, quickly!"

For a moment he said nothing. Then, "Do you know what you're asking?" he demanded. "How can I betray my comrades, the Red Army, everything I believe in!"

"Not betray, *not* betray," I whispered, tears rolling down my cheeks. "Does your revolution stand for cold-blooded murder? Is there no mercy in it?" I twisted Anastasia's ring off my finger. "This is Anastasia's. Take it to the Whites, Kolya. Tell them whose it is, and beg them to come before it's too late!" I pressed it into his hand and folded his fingers around it.

He gave me a despairing look, then thrust his hand into his pocket, and walked away.

Sick at heart, I lay awake all night. What had I

done? Would Kolya betray me to Yurovsky? No, he'd never do that. But would he go to the Whites at all? And if he did, would they believe him? Then a terrible thought crossed my mind. They might shoot him! For wasn't he a Red soldier? *Do you know what you're asking?* he'd said. I buried my face in my pillow.

The next day Yurovsky's troops took over the Ipatiev house. At first the family thought they were an improvement. They brought back some of our belongings, which the other troops had pilfered, and Yurovsky sent eggs and milk to improve Alexei's diet. He even promised the Tsarina that he would allow a priest to hold a religious service for them soon.

He couldn't fool me. He just wanted to keep us quiet until he was ready.

"What's the matter with you? You're acting so strange lately," complained Anastasia.

But they began to feel it, too, the deadly cold that radiated from Yurovsky. Soon he had iron bars put over the open window.

"I like this fellow less and less," muttered the Tsar.

The next day there were revolver shots in the distance. We heard the sound of marching feet and the jingle of cavalry passing by.

"The Whites must be getting closer," whispered Anastasia. I thought of Kolya, and prayed.

The day after, Yurovsky granted the Tsarina the religious service she had yearned for, and it seemed to comfort her. But in the middle of it Olga suddenly began to sob. Tatiana put her arms around her, and Olga leaned her head against Tatiana's shoulder.

We are walking beneath God, I thought.

After supper, the Tsar sat in his favourite chair. "I don't think I can read aloud tonight," he said, rubbing his eyes. The electricity had gone off that afternoon, and all we had was the evening light behind the whitewashed windows.

"Remember when Dunia used to tell us stories?" said Alexei, who was lying on a sofa. "Tell us one now, Dunia."

"Yes!" said Anastasia. "And we can all imagine we're back at Tsarskoe."

"Ah, Tsarskoe!" sighed the Tsarina.

"But which story do you want?" I asked.

"The one about the brave tsarevich," said Alexei, settling himself against his pillows.

"All tsareviches are brave, aren't they?" I said. And he gave me a smile.

"I remember the one he means. There's a warrior queen in it," said Anastasia.

"And a princess who married a raven," said Marie.

"Oh, 'Maria Morevna,'" I said, settling myself cross-legged on the rug. And then my Anastasia did something she had never done before. She slipped down beside me and put her head in my lap.

"Once, long ago, there was a brave tsarevich," I began, stroking her hair. "And he had four beautiful sisters."

"That's right!" Alexei nodded.

"And one day a raven spoke to him and asked to marry the eldest . . . " And so I spun a web of words around my dear ones in the long summer twilight.

23

Windows

July 16 – July 25, 1918

I was slicing black bread in the kitchen the next morning when Yurovsky tramped in and told the guards to take Lyonka away. The poor boy squealed like a rabbit struck by a hawk.

"Stop that noise!" said Yurovsky. "Your uncle is here. Don't you want to see him?" Then, "You too," he added, turning to me.

"No!" I said. "I won't go!" Brandishing the bread knife, I kicked the shins of the first guard who laid hands on me, but a second twisted my wrist until I dropped the knife. Then he pinned my arms behind me and pushed me out the door. "No!" I cried again, as they bundled me down the stairs. A hand was clapped over my mouth. Behind me, I heard Anastasia's voice from the dining room cry out, "Dunia? *Dunia!*"

Downstairs, Yurovsky pressed the cold barrel of his revolver to my cheek. "You don't want to scream and upset the family, do you?" I shook my head, and he took the gun away. The other took his hand off my mouth, and I spat out the taste of him.

"We're only taking you to the Popov house next door," Yurovsky said. "You'll be better off there. I hear you're a soldier's sweetheart," he added, grinning. But his eyes were cold.

Did he know about Kolya, then. Had they caught him? Or . . . Had he never gone at all?

I stared back at the Ipatiev house as they marched us next door, but saw only the eyeless plank fence. In the Popov house, they flung us into a small closet on the ground floor.

Yurovsky stared down at me. "You will stay here and make no noise at all," he said softly. "If you know what's good for you." Then he slammed the door. We heard a key grate in the lock, and then footsteps going away. We were left in the stuffy darkness.

"Where's my uncle?" whined Lyonka. "They said I'd be seeing my uncle."

"Oh, be quiet!" I snapped. I put my head down on my knees and tried to think. I had to get out, I had to get back to them. Had to, had to, had to. After awhile, I crawled over to the door and felt about. There was a knob on the inside, but turning it did no good. The door was locked.

Hours passed, and the closet grew hotter and hotter. I heard a sudden clatter of boots on the stairs and in the hall. They must be changing the guard, I thought. Lyonka had cried himself to sleep, and I almost slipped into a doze. Then a tiny sound caught my ear and I jerked wide awake. Someone was turning the key in the lock! Holding my breath, I waited for the door to open, but it didn't. Then I heard a voice whisper, "Take your chance, little sister. The guards are eating, and the front door unlocked." Then I heard footsteps going away.

I turned the handle and the door opened. I gave Lyonka a shake. "Someone has unlocked the door," I whispered. "I'm going back to the Ipatiev house. Are you coming?"

"I'm afraid," he faltered. "And they told me my uncle is here."

"God be with you then," I said, and opened the door a crack. It was as my mysterious saviour had said — the front hall was deserted. I could hear the sound of voices from the far end of the hall, and the air smelled of boiled cabbage. I ran down the hall and slipped out the front door. Where now? I wondered, glancing both ways to make sure that no one had noticed me. Not across the square to the Ipatiev house — I'd run straight into the guards. I'd have to take a longer way around. So I turned away from the square and plunged down the first lane I came to.

It was evening, but still light. I'd have to find somewhere to hide until dark. I heard low grunting from a garden right beside me, and caught an unmistakable whiff of pig. Well, I'd had worse companions. I whisked over the low wooden fence, and slipped into the sty. The sow inside snorted, but made no other protest. It was munching kitchen scraps from a trough.

"Thanks, sister," I said, as I filled my pockets with the best bits. For who knew how long I'd have to hide?

Chewing a bruised apple, I settled myself to wait for dark. Who had set me free? Was it because of Kolya? And now I was free, how could I get back to the family?

At last it grew so dark that I could hardly see my hand in front of my face. I slipped back over the fence and made my way along the lane, flitting in and out of doorways and into shadowy corners until I was opposite the garden wall of the Ipatiev house. A guard was pacing back and forth outside it, and I knew there was another inside the garden.

The guard reached the far corner of the wall, and stopped to talk with another sentry. One of them struck a match while the other cupped his hands around it and leaned forward to light a cigarette. For a minute, they wouldn't see anything! I dashed across the street and flung myself at the wall. Wedging my fingers and toes between the stones, I swarmed up it. At the top, I dropped into the garden and crouched behind some bushes, listening. Had the garden sentry seen me?

I heard voices behind the house. The guards on the second-floor terrace were calling orders to a man below. I glanced toward the left side of the yard. There was a shed between the bath house and the root cellar. If I could reach it . . .

I slunk along the wall of the bath house. The shed door sagged ajar, and I slipped inside. Peering out, I saw the sentry hurrying across the yard. Had he spotted me? But no, he went into the summer house instead.

"Get up, you lazy dog," I heard him shout. "This is no time to sleep it off. We've work to do tonight!" There was a grunt of protest, and then two figures headed for the house, one prodding the other, who stumbled ahead of him.

There was no more noise from the guards. The bells of the church across the square chimed eleven. Upstairs, lights winked off in the maid's room and the kitchen. The family must have gone to bed too. Scratching some straw together, I settled down on it to wait. It was chilly, and I shivered as I tried to think what to do next. Tomorrow, when the family came outdoors for exercise, I could at least signal to Anastasia, to let her know I was there. And perhaps help was already on the way. If only Kolya . . . But had he gone to the Whites? I put my head down on my knees.

The bells chimed for midnight . . . for one o'clock . . . Far away, a dog barked. And then I heard the sound of a truck. I got up and went to the door of the shed. Headlights swept the plank fence on the side where the gate was. A door slammed, and I heard voices. Suddenly, lights began to be turned on until the whole house was ablaze.

What was happening? More time passed. Then I heard footsteps, as if people were walking along the side of the house inside the plank fence. Minutes later came the roar of many revolvers firing. I heard a woman scream, and the firing went on and on . . . Then came a terrible silence.

Trembling, I clung to the door of the shed. Had they shot the Tsar, then, and the Tsarina? We had feared that for so long! Please, no . . . Tears flowed down my face, and I bit the back of my hand to keep from sobbing aloud.

But . . . They wouldn't have hurt the children, I tried to comfort myself. Surely they wouldn't. What harm could the children do to the Revolution? The Tsarina herself had said that even if she and the Tsar were harmed, they wouldn't hurt the children . . . What would happen to them now? I thought of them clinging together, grief-stricken, and crossed myself. "Dear Lord, give them the strength to bear it," I prayed. Somehow I'd find a way to get to them, to go with them wherever they were sent. If the guards wouldn't let me, they'd have to kill me too!

Minutes later, I heard the truck drive away. But the guards remained at their posts. The lights stayed on all night, and I heard much coming and going at the door to the lower floor, but saw nothing. Near dawn, sick at heart, I curled up on my patch of straw and slept.

The next day, no one came into the garden for exercise, or the next. But lights were turned on in the house at the usual time, and I could see smoke from the kitchen chimney. The children *were* still there — they must be! — and Kharitonov was preparing food for them, I told myself.

As for me, I was hungry indeed, for I had long

since eaten all the pig scraps. But I discovered some mouldy potatoes in a sack, and there was water in the rain barrel by the shed. With this I had to be content. Slowly I drifted into a strange state, half waking, half sleeping. I dreamed often of my mother, and felt her close to me. It comforted me a little.

Days later, I heard the shouting of orders in the streets, and the guards suddenly disappeared. Then came the sound of many trucks driving away. Were the Reds leaving Ekaterinburg? Were they taking the children, or had they left them behind?

I stumbled across the yard and tried to climb the wall. But I was too weak now. So I dragged a garden chair over. Standing on it, I hauled myself to the top of the wall and dropped to the ground, landing painfully on my hands and knees.

I got up and ran along the plank fence, ducking through the first gate I came to. Then a blur of brown and white raced up and flung itself on me. "Joy!" I cried, for it was Alexei's spaniel. He would never have left Joy behind. The children *were* still here!

"Where are they, Joy?" I gasped, "Where?"

The dog whined, and ran over to the side door. I turned the knob and it swung open. The room ahead of me was empty. Joy ran across it and disappeared through another door. I followed, then stopped, drawing in my breath sharply. This room, too, was empty, but one wall was riddled with bullet holes, which had blasted away great chunks of plaster. The floor was slashed and gouged as if by bayonets. Yet it was all eerily clean and neat, and I could smell the sharp tang of soap. Something terrible had happened here — the air still shuddered with it.

"Blessed Saviour!" I gasped, crossing myself. Joy had stopped in the middle of the room. Now he lay down on the floor and put his head on his paws. "Come, Joy," I called, backing away. He whined, but he wouldn't follow me.

I ran up the kitchen stairs at the back of the house. "It's me, Dunia!" I shouted. But there was no reply. Kharitonov's neat kitchen was wrecked, with pots and pans tumbled from their shelves and dishes smashed on the floor. There had been no cooking here. Yet the stove was choked with ashes.

"Anastasia?" I cried. "Alexei?"

The dining room and the salon were the same as the kitchen, stoves stuffed with scorched paper, floors strewn with smashed icons, torn books, broken picture frames. The Tsarina's empty wheelchair stood ghost-like in a doorway, a silent witness to the ruin, and all the whitewashed windows of their prison were flung open wide. I trod on something and picked it up. It was Anastasia's hairbrush, half-burnt. But she would have taken that if she had to go away!

My heart grew cold within me then, and at last I understood what the little dog grieving downstairs already knew. My dear ones were gone from me forever. They were all of them gone out of this world where I couldn't follow.

I sank to my knees. "Anastasia," I whispered. The summer breeze fanned my cheek, stirring the ashes that spilled from the stove in the corner. A scrap of paper tumbled across the floor, and I picked it up. It was my snapshot of Anastasia on the beach at Livadia. It was badly charred, but I could still see her laughing face, and behind her Alexei's last sand castle crumbling into the sea.

Epilogue

Koptyaki Wood

Spring, 1926

It is spring, and the birch trees burn with the tiny green flames of their new leaves. I take the road through the woods beyond the town, and cross the railway tracks. Not far beyond, I stop at a certain place. For I know a secret, one that only a few others share.

Our Soviet government has admitted at last that Yurovsky and his men shot all who were in the Ipatiev house that night — Tsar, Tsarina, children and servants alike. The newspaper even published Yurovsky's report. He ordered the family downstairs, he said. He told them he was going to take their photograph, and arranged them in two rows. Then he and his men opened fire. When there were no more bullets, there were bayonets. . . . After it was over, they washed down the walls and the floor with soap, removing every trace of blood. The bodies were taken to Koptyaki Wood, where they were burned to ashes and scattered to the winds.

Yurovsky lies. Oh, they killed and they tried to burn, yes. But they couldn't destroy the evidence of their terrible crime. So they buried their victims in another part of the wood. Here. There is nothing to mark the spot, and we who visit in secret wish for nothing. For if the government suspected that some of us know the truth, they would open the grave and try to hide the evidence elsewhere. No, let the dead rest in peace.

I come not often — I dare not — but always in the spring, to bring Anastasia a handful of the violets she loved. I bury my nose in them, breathing in their musty sweetness, and think of the woods at Tsarskoe Selo, and the violets like a blue mist under the trees. It seems like a dream.

The White Army captured Ekaterinburg eight days after that terrible night in the Ipatiev house. Too late, too late! Officers of the White Army found me in the house, and questioned me. When they had heard my story, they took me to where they kept their prisoners. A tall brown-haired boy looked out at me through the bars.

"Kolya!" I cried. For I had feared that he was dead.

"They wouldn't believe me, Dunia," he said sadly. "They said I had stolen the ring, and that the Reds were setting a trap for them."

When they knew the truth, the Whites set him free, but Kolya refused to join them. "I must go to the Red Army," he told me. "They may shoot me for what I tried to do. If they don't, I'll fight for the Revolution. Will you come with me or stay?"

"I must stay," I said, for I knew that my heart was in this place forever. "Oh, Kolya, please come back."

And so he went away. I found a job in a factory — they were short-handed now that so many workers had run away with the Reds. Months later, I was plodding home when a big car stopped beside me.

"Dunia?" called a familiar voice. It was Zhilik. He and Gibbsy had been asked by the Whites to help investigate what had happened to the Tsar and Tsarina. I told them all I knew. And when the snow melted in the spring, they took the three of us to the terrible place in Koptyaki Wood where Yurovsky and his murderers had tried to destroy the evidence of their crime. We found the ashes of many fires, and, ground deep into the churned-up earth all around, bits of precious things — the Tsar's belt buckle, one of the Tsarina's pearl earrings and a broken fragment of an emerald cross. One group of objects had puzzled the investigators, a mixture of nails, tinfoil, copper coins and a small lock. Zhilik, Gibbsy and I wept. It was Alexei's collection of useful things.

We stood in frozen silence while they searched a nearby mine shaft. They found more telltale fragments, and at the bottom of the pit, the corpse of Anastasia's little Jimmy. But they didn't find the family, and they never did.

But the peasants of Koptyaki Village knew every glade of the wood. They saw a spot where railway ties had suddenly appeared in the muddy road. They lifted them and found . . .

The peasants said nothing to the Whites, of

course, or to the Reds when they recaptured Ekaterinburg the following summer. Yet somehow the word spread to a few who needed to know the truth.

When the Reds defeated the Whites at last, Kolya came home. We got married, and I found a better job, taking photographs. Even commissars like having their pictures taken. And so we work, we eat and sleep, and work again, and hope that some day our children will have a better life. When I do have children I will tell them stories, my mother's and my own. And this one, which is true, yet stranger by far than all the rest.

Though the Bolsheviks say we are free now, some people grumble that nothing has really changed, that we have new Red tsars ruling over us. What will be cannot be escaped, folk say.

They still whisper about the Tsar and his family. Only the Tsar was shot, some insist. The Tsarina and her children were spared. Others say they have glimpsed Alexei in this village, or Tatiana in that. Strangest of all, some believe that all the Romanovs are still alive, sailing on a yacht around the polar sea, never touching land, and that some day they will come back to us.

I know the truth — or thought I did, until today. For while I was folding a piece of newspaper to cover a hole in my shoe, I saw a photograph and a headline with the name *Anastasia*. A woman has appeared in Germany, the story said, falsely claiming to be the Grand Duchess Anastasia Nikolaevna. My heart missed a beat. *Falsely*, like all the other pretenders? Or . . .

I take the newspaper photograph out of my pocket. The grainy image stares back at me. Could it be? *Could* it? So many years have passed, she would have changed . . .

I lay the bunch of violets on the ground, and look up at the shafts of golden sunlight slanting between the birches. Oh, my malenkaya, my little one, my dear! If it *is* you, if you are alive, may you know that one loving heart is loyal still.

But then, you always knew that, my Anastasia.

Eclipse Photography

Sharon Stewart has always been interested in writing, and has combined this with her love of history to create popular and historically accurate fiction for young readers. Her longtime interest in European history, and her fascination with the French Revolution, led her to create the story of Marie Thérèse, daughter of Marie Antoinette, in *The Dark Tower*, which was shortlisted for the Geoffrey Bilson Award for Historical Fiction. Then she went on to explore the life of another tragic princess in *My Anastasia*.

Sharon lives in Toronto, but worked on *My Anastasia* in Navarra, Spain while her husband was there on a year-long teaching assignment. She is the author of *The Dark Tower*, *The Minstrel Boy* and *Spider's Web*.